"Now, Miss Retro I[...] you going to laugh at my riding skills again?"

Vy stalked to the edge of the stream, hot and bothered and struggling to get herself under control.

She felt Sam's heat behind her.

"Now that we've acknowledged our attraction to each other, do you want to tell me why you hate me so much?"

"You're a phony," she said. "You're no more a cowboy than I am."

"Considering how obvious it is that I can't even fake it well, yes. I am a phony. I have my reasons."

She rounded on him. Big mistake. His nearness, his height, his insightful gray eyes disconcerted her.

Damn. She wasn't used to being out of control. She was the one people came to for her cool head under pressure.

What was this man doing to her?

Dear Reader,

I have so much fun writing about the cowboys and children in my stories, and in particular, about those in the small town of fictitious Rodeo, Montana.

As I moved along in this series, I wondered how the townspeople would react to a man who comes to town pretending to be a cowboy when it's painfully obvious that he isn't one!

How would a certain diner owner, who's been hurt by a phony in her past, be affected?

Sam and Violet's story blossomed out of that idea and raised so many questions. Why on earth would a normally intelligent city man decide it was a good idea to pretend to be a cowboy? How did he think he could possibly pull it off?

The answer to the second question is that he doesn't. He is found out immediately.

The answer to the first question is the strongest motivator of all—love for a very dear grandfather. All of his ill-fated decisions were made to protect a man he adores.

Sam's biggest mistake is in thinking that the six women, including Violet, who are reviving the local rodeo and amusement park to save their small town, could possibly be dishonest and cheating his grandfather. It's a huge assumption that takes Sam most of the story to realize is all wrong, but along the way he falls for spirited, opinionated Violet.

I hope you enjoy their story.

Mary Sullivan

RODEO BABY

——

Mary Sullivan

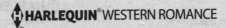

HARLEQUIN® WESTERN ROMANCE

Recycling programs
for this product may
not exist in your area.

ISBN-13: 978-0-373-75768-8

Rodeo Baby

Copyright © 2017 by Mary Sullivan

Printed in U.S.A.

www.Harlequin.com

Mary Sullivan has a fondness for cowboys and ranch settings, even though she grew up in the city. She found her mother's stories about growing up in rural Canada fascinating. Her passions outside of writing include time spent with friends, great conversation, exploring her city, cooking, walking, traveling (including her latest trip to Paris!), reading, meeting readers and doing endless crossword puzzles.

She loves to hear from readers and can be reached through her website at marysullivanbooks.com, or via her Facebook author page, Facebook.com/marysullivanauthor.

Books by Mary Sullivan

Harlequin Western Romance

Rodeo Father
Rodeo Rancher

Harlequin Superromance

No Ordinary Sheriff
In from the Cold
Home to Laura
Because of Audrey
Always Emily
No Ordinary Home
Safe in Noah's Arms
Cody's Come Home

Visit the Author Profile page
at Harlequin.com for more titles.

To Susan, who has become a very dear friend.

Chapter One

The second Violet Summer laid eyes on the stranger, an unreasonable swell of sexual awareness bloomed.

The man wasn't even her type, yet here she stood stunned, and bothered, with Lester Voile's coffee and Mama's Best Meat Loaf cooling in her hands.

Rats.

Rodeo, and the Summertime Diner, rarely saw anyone like the stranger sliding into the second booth from the front door—suave, urbane…and dressed like a cowboy?

If he'd ever ridden out on the range, Vy would eat an old boot.

He looked like a movie star acting the role of a cowboy but not playing him well.

She chronicled every detail, including the neatly ironed jeans. What cowboy worth his salt ironed his jeans? How many decades had it been since *anyone* ironed jeans?

Vy started toward his booth.

He set his cowboy hat, sweat-free and spotless, on the table in front of him. Sunlight streaming through the window shot rays through his golden hair. His strong, clean-shaven jaw sent shivers through her.

Even knowing he was too slick and polished to be a real cowboy, she found him attractive, deep in her gut where reaction came before thought.

No, he was *not* her type, but good grief, just what she needed—an instant attraction to an imitation cowboy. As if she didn't have enough to worry about these days.

Irritated, she plunked Lester Voile's meal on his table.

Ignoring Lester's muttered thanks, she approached the stranger's booth, self-protective instincts on high alert.

Why, Vy? He's just a guy who's dropped into your diner. A stranger. You know nothing about him. There's nothing to protect yourself from.

Except her own unruly attraction.

She pulled out her notepad and waited, giving the stranger a minute to adjust to her presence. He knew she was there. As she'd approached, he'd checked out her legs from under his blond lashes.

He set aside the menu and looked up. With that blond hair, she'd expected blue eyes, not the deep, cool gray that studied her.

He smiled, his grin broad and confident. Good Lord, the man had dimples and used them to good effect.

Well, he could grin all day long. She was immune. Plus his smile didn't reach his eyes, so it was just charm, not innate good humor or character, which she valued a heck of a lot more than personality.

Or, Vy, maybe he's in a bad mood and trying to rise above it. Don't make assumptions. People do have them, y'know. You've seen enough people come into the diner when their lives were low to not take it personally. Don't do it now. Park your paranoia in your apron pocket and do your job.

She asked, "Can I take your order?"

"I'll have the World's Best Cheeseburger with everything but onions." Why did he have to have a melodious, deep voice that spoke to Vy's longings? She hardened her defenses.

She had her hands full running the diner, not to mention pulling together all of the concession stands for the revived fair and rodeo at the end of August.

Handsome men were not on her agenda.

Slowly, the man pulled his eyes away from hers and said, "What do you want, honey?"

Huh? What did *she* want? And who was he calling honey—

A young voice to her right spoke. Vy glanced toward the other bench of the high-backed booth.

Oh. He wasn't alone. How had she missed that?

A young girl glared at the man. She couldn't be more than twelve, maybe thirteen, cloaked in not only enough black punk accessories to build body armor but also plenty of baby fat and attitude. Straight white teeth and a flawless complexion hinted at beauty in development. The kid would be a knockout someday, despite her current wardrobe.

Vy had learned early to be a quick judge of character. Unless she missed her guess, the kid belonged in a prep school somewhere, not in a diner in a small town pretending to be tough.

Vy knew a lost baby chick when she saw one.

She used to be one.

"Chelsea, I'll ask only one more time," the man said, voice thick with forced patience. "What will you have for lunch?"

When the girl crossed her arms with a mulish jut of her jaw and refused to respond, the man ordered for her. "My daughter will also have a cheeseburger, but top hers with plenty of onions."

"Daaad." Chelsea sat up straight. "You *know* I *hate* onions."

He held up one finger. "Then the next time I ask you

a question not once but twice, you'll do me the courtesy of responding."

Hmm… With many of the fathers she knew, local cowboys and ranchers, the conversation would have gone something like "When I ask a question, you answer. Got it?" Nothing as refined as "You'll do me the courtesy of responding."

Vy bit back a smile. This fake cowboy gave himself away at every turn.

To Vy, he said, "We'll both have fries with the burgers. I'll have a coffee and my daughter will have a glass of milk."

"But I want a soda." Again with the whiny voice.

"Goes back to what I said earlier. I ask and you respond." His attention swinging back to Vy, he held on to his grin desperately, but cracks in the wall of his charm showed. "Bring her milk."

"Got it." She pointed to his cowboy hat. "No need to leave your hat on the table."

She indicated the hooks that lined the walls on both sides of the front door.

"Wouldn't want you to spill anything on your spotless, brand-spanking-new hat."

Laughing, she returned to the kitchen, glad to leave the tension coiled at the table like a rattlesnake. She regretted that they'd wandered into her diner. She welcomed all business, but not the heartache on that poor girl's face and the fissures in the careful facade of the father's cultured shell.

The man looked like he belonged more in the Tradition Golf and Country Club way up the highway in Festival than he did in the Summertime Diner in Rodeo, but who they were and what they were doing here were none of her business or concern.

Ha. As if you could ever keep your nose out of other people's business.

Vy grinned and turned her attention to picking up orders.

SAM CARMICHAEL, aka Sam Michaels, watched the waitress walk away, the sway of her nicely rounded hips captivating.

Her nametag read "Violet," a soft, old-fashioned name for a woman with intelligence and cheekiness snapping in her gaze.

Violet Summer.

One of the five.

No, at last count there were six of *them*, the people who were reviving his grandfather's amusement park, the people he'd come here to investigate. Using Gramps's fairgrounds, five local women planned to stage a fair and a rodeo at the end of the summer. Recently they'd added a newcomer, an accountant, to their team.

They had leased Gramps's land for one dollar and a handshake.

No contract.

Sam was here to make sure Gramps wasn't being taken for a ride.

The waitress—a damned good-looking woman with jet hair, clear skin and a retro fifties' tight bodice and flared skirt—entered the kitchen, cutting off his view of her.

She had purple eyes. No, to be more accurate, he'd say *violet*, purple softened with a hint of gray. He'd never seen a color like them.

Or maybe he had. Elizabeth Taylor had purple eyes. As a boy, he used to enjoy watching old movies with his mother, but he'd never seen such an unusual color in the flesh before.

Were they real? Could they be contacts?

His fascination with the woman overcame his pique with his daughter's incessant, grinding resistance.

Chelsea slumped low in the booth across from him.

Sure, divorce took its toll on kids, but it had been a full year since he and Tiffany had signed the papers, and more than a year and a half since Tiff had said, "I've met someone else. I want a divorce," gutting Sam.

Standing, he sighed. Nineteen to twenty months wasn't nearly long enough to process betrayal and greed. Tiffany's, not his.

While his daily mantra ran through his head—*success is the best revenge*—he hung his hat where the waitress had indicated, then returned to his table, nodding to the old guy two booths away eating meat loaf and mashed potatoes.

The man, ancient and wrinkled, eyed him suspiciously.

This diner and the bar at the end of the street called Honey's Place were the only eating establishments as far as he could tell.

Guess they were stuck with diner food with corny names. World's Best Cheeseburger…

The diner could have been picked up and plunked down in any fifties' town. He was surprised there weren't Elvis and Chuck Berry songs blaring from jukeboxes.

Deep red leather banquettes framed gray Formica tables. Red-and-white-checked cotton place mats sat at the ready.

The paintings on the wall came as a surprise. He expected nostalgic black-and-white photos but instead saw rustic, wild landscapes. Were the artist and scenery local? He couldn't deny they were good. He also couldn't deny the scenery around this little town was spectacular.

"Why can't we use our own names?" Chelsea picked at her peeling nail polish. He wished she'd quit with the unrelieved black. "Why do we have to pretend to be other people?"

"Shush." Sam shot a glance around the diner. No one seemed to have heard Chelsea's remark, thank goodness. "We have to be Sam and Chelsea Michaels so I can determine what's going on about the rodeo."

"Why don't you just ask?"

She's still so young, he reminded himself, *and so naive.*

"I don't trust people to be honest."

"Maybe you should. Maybe we aren't all the creeps you think we are."

He stilled. "You actually believe I think you're a creep?" he whispered, unable to mask the hurt that coursed through him. Hadn't he proved his love all of the times in her childhood he'd held her and told her how much he loved her?

She shrugged. Love her or not, he'd come to hate her shrugs as much as her eye rolls. Double for the word *duh.* And *d'oh.*

The waitress returned. Black eyeliner tilted up at the corners of her eyes and deep red lipstick emphasized lush lips. She fit right in with the decor. Did she have to dress in that fifties's fashion?

The style suited her spectacular figure, emphasizing generous hips, a tiny waist and full breasts. The lush proportions worked, reminiscent again of Elizabeth Taylor.

Give your head a shake. For Gramps's sake, it wasn't wise to find her attractive. She was one of them. Once he determined how the women resurrecting the local fair were ripping off his grandfather, he would shut them down and move back east.

The sooner he could get back to New York to set up his next business venture, the better.

Careful, his rational, less emotional side cautioned. *You*

need to first determine if they are indeed cheating him.
But that one-dollar lease disturbed him.

The waitress put his plate in front of him and then Chelsea's in front of her. He couldn't smell onions on Chelsea's burger, but that meant nothing. There were so many scents in the diner he wasn't sure he would be able to.

Chelsea peeked under the top of the hamburger bun. A tiny, mean-spirited smile that usually meant trouble formed at one corner of her mouth.

Sam braced himself. Where had his sweet daughter gone and who was this stranger now in possession of her body? Apparently, once a girl turned thirteen, demons took over.

He glanced at the waitress. "You wouldn't happen to know where the closest exorcist lives, would you?"

Violet smiled—even, white teeth framed by cherry red. "We're plumb out. We burned the last one at the stake with all of our witches a hundred years back."

Sam stared. She'd gotten his joke! His ex-wife's reaction had always been a frown because she hadn't understood his humor. Chelsea used to get his jokes but had become too cool to laugh or even smile. He'd grown used to their negativity. The waitress's willingness to play along was pure pleasure. He perked up.

She jerked her chin toward his daughter. "It's surprising what a good cheeseburger will do to expel demons."

Chelsea took her time looking over the waitress insolently. Apparently, once she'd become a teenager, she'd lost all of the good manners that had been drummed into her throughout her short childhood.

"You dress funny," she said with a snicker.

"Chelsea!"

Violet leaned one hand on the table and rested her other on her hip. "So do you."

Chelsea scowled. "You're only a waitress. You can't talk to me like that."

"When you are rude to me, I can respond in any way I please. If you don't like it, you can leave. Are you going to eat your meal or should I take it away?"

"I'll eat." Sam detected grudging respect in Chelsea's tone.

The waitress straightened away from the table. "Take the silver spoon out of your mouth first so you don't choke."

A grudging smile bloomed on Chelsea's face.

How did the woman know they had money? To fit in, Sam had dressed down in denim and a plaid shirt, along with cowboy boots and hat.

Chelsea wore black punk. What about them said money? Nothing, as far as he could tell. He had to be more careful. The woman's intuition disturbed him and he struck out at her.

"I asked you to load her burger with onions." He hadn't really wanted the waitress to, but Chelsea had many lessons to learn and Sam had no patience left for teaching them. Every stop on this ill-conceived trip, every mile of highway traveled across country and every single black inch of asphalt navigated had been littered with heartache for both of them. When all roads had steep uphill pitches, all you wanted was to roll backward and give up.

He wished he could turn back time and start over with his daughter.

Violet flipped her violet gaze on Sam. "Do you want her to eat or not?"

"At this point, I don't much care," he groused. Tired, hungry and out of patience, he wished he was back home in Manhattan where he belonged.

"Mom says I shouldn't eat too much," his child piped up. "She says I'm too fat."

"You're not fat!" Sam hadn't meant to raise his voice, but Tiffany's complaints about Chelsea had worn him thin. "You're perfect, okay?"

"You should eat, kid." The waitress smelled like fried food and roses.

Sam held his breath. Nobody called Chelsea a kid and got away with it. On her young, chubby face, thunder started to build.

Then Violet added, "It takes a lot of calories to feed that much 'tude."

Chelsea burst out laughing, stunning Sam. His daughter, who hadn't laughed in months, who hadn't given him a genuine smile in twice that long, picked up her burger and happily bit into it.

Violet sauntered away while Sam envisioned himself getting down on his knees and kissing her feet...and every inch of her calves. She had great calves, strong but feminine.

She returned with their drinks.

"Has anyone ever mentioned that your name matches your eyes?" They were gorgeous.

"Nope. Not once. That's a new one." She slapped cream and sugar onto the table in front of him.

His jaw hardened. She had no right to treat him badly. It was just mild harmless flirtation. "*You've* got a lot of attitude." He didn't like sarcasm. Didn't like people treating him badly. Back home—

Well, he wasn't back home, was he?

"Let me speak to the manager," he ordered.

"That would be me."

"Okay, then. Is the owner in?"

She tapped one red-tipped fingernail against her chin. "Let me think. Yes. That would also be me."

Chelsea giggled.

Good Lord. Two against one. "You don't know much about business and good customer service, do you?"

He'd meant to put her in her place, but she turned to the customers in the large room and called out, "Does anyone have trouble with how I run my business?"

One and all shook their heads no.

Damn. He hadn't meant to draw attention.

"Do I give good customer service or not?"

"Good service, Vy," the old guy two tables down yelled. "Love the mashed potatoes. What did you say you put in them?"

"Garlic, Lester. That's why they're called garlic mashed potatoes."

"Makes sense." Lester nodded. "Like 'em. Refill my coffee when you get a minute?"

"Sure thing. I'll get right on it as soon as I can get away from this table."

Heat in Sam's cheeks burned. His daughter watched him with a mocking smile. The townspeople watched him curiously. Great. He'd wanted to avoid drawing attention to himself, but here he was center stage because of this bad-tempered woman.

She presented her back to him and walked away.

"All I did was be nice to her," he mumbled while he doctored his coffee.

"You gave her your fake, cheesy grin, Dad. You were flirting with her badly."

He pinned his daughter with a hard glare. "What do you know about flirting?"

She rolled her eyes. Sick of the action, he pulled out of his pocket a small change purse he'd picked up at a souvenir shop on the way. "You rolled your eyes. Pay up."

"Daaad."

"Pay up." He held out the purse. "Now."

She took a quarter out of her pink knapsack and dropped it into the change purse.

"It's getting heavy," he remarked.

"You're mean to take money away from your daughter. I'm only thirteen years old!"

"Thirteen going on twenty. Your mother gave you all kinds of money before we left. I give you a good allowance. You ain't starving, kid."

"Aren't. It's *aren't* starving. Just because we're in this tiny town doesn't mean you have to speak like the locals."

Sam grinned, but didn't apologize. "What was wrong with my flirting with the waitress?"

"Owner."

"Owner," he conceded.

"You're coming on way too strong. It makes you sound corny. Maybe you forget how to do it right because you're getting old."

He bristled. "Since when is thirty-nine old?"

She shrugged.

A minute later, he said, "There's nothing wrong with flirting. It's what men and women do when they're attracted to each other."

"I know, but don't be so artificial about it." She mimicked him with a false voice, "'Your violet eyes match your name,'" and, worse, with a fake smile. She looked like a politician.

"Her eyes *do* match her name." Defensiveness made him petulant.

"Yeah, and that's *so* obvious. Everybody must say that to her. You have to notice different things and say more original stuff."

"Like what?"

"She's funny. She makes me laugh."

"At my expense. I'm not about to compliment her on her

sense of humor when I'm the butt of her jokes." He liked her legs, especially her calves.

"So should I have said, 'Great calves, lady'? Yeah, that would have gone over real well."

Chelsea peered around the edge of the booth to look at Violet's legs as she stood chatting with customers at another table. The girl turned back to him with wide eyes. "Her calves are kind of big. You think they're great?"

"Sure. They're shapely."

The thoughtful frown on Chelsea's forehead intrigued him.

"There's nothing wrong with a woman being shapely."

She nodded, still thoughtful.

"I wasn't kidding, Chelsea. You are perfect the way you are. Your mom stressed too much about being thin."

"So, like, didn't you like her that thin?"

"I wouldn't have minded if she worried about it less. It was always on her mind. She ate like a bird."

"Not really, Dad. Lots of birds eat half their body weight every day."

He smiled slowly because Chelsea was smiling, too. When she was small, they seemed to have this ability to read each other's minds and get each other's jokes before they'd even been delivered. "Can you imagine your mom eating half her body weight?"

She laughed then sobered. "She used to binge and purge."

Sam's lips thinned. "Purge. You mean…"

Chelsea sighed. "Yeah. Didn't you know? Mom used to get rid of her food after dinner all the time."

He'd known, of course—she was painfully thin—but had hoped Chelsea had remained ignorant. It seemed she'd been aware all along.

Kids always did seem to know everything you tried to hide from them.

He wanted his daughter to have healthy behavior.

"Chelsea, promise me something?"

She made a noncommittal sound, which he took as permission to continue. "Never do that. Okay? Never. Enjoy your food and your life. Nothing is worth that kind of behavior. It didn't buy your mother more love or more respect. Okay?"

"Yeah." She stared at the fry in her hand. "Okay."

"Eat up." He picked up his burger.

On her way along to another customer, Violet slapped a bowl of ketchup onto their table.

What was her problem?

He was a paying customer like everyone else in the diner and deserved as much respect, but she'd taken an instant dislike to him.

Or maybe it was you trying to get her into trouble with her manager, Sam, who just happened to be her.

Starving, he bit into his burger and instantly sat up straight.

"This is good." He wiped juice from his chin. "Excellent."

"Yeah. It's the best burger I've had since we left home."

"No fooling." It was the best he'd had in years.

"The fries are good, too," Chelsea said.

He bit into one, twice fried so they were crispy. Vinegar and pepper sharpened the side dish of coleslaw.

Maybe eating here wouldn't be so bad, after all, if the rest of the meals lived up to their corny names.

For the first time since leaving home, he felt in harmony with his daughter. He'd missed that amazing feeling.

A craving arose in him to relax with her and have fun

like he used to do, to tease her and hug her and call her goofy pet names.

He didn't want to be this uptight guy he'd become since Tiffany's betrayal.

On impulse, he blurted, "Let's share dessert?"

She brightened a little. "Okay."

They argued for a good five minutes about what they would share.

"I'm too full to eat a whole dessert," he said.

"Me, too."

"So we have to come to an agreement. We do that by negotiation."

"Dad, I hate when you *teach* me. Why can't we just talk?"

"I thought we were just talking."

"No, you're lecturing and I'm—"

They were interrupted by Violet plopping a plate in the middle of the table with small portions of four desserts and two forks.

"Knock yourselves out," she said. She slapped their bill onto the table and walked away. He checked the total. Too reasonable. She needed to raise the price points on her meals.

"She heard us arguing." Chelsea stared at the plate before picking up a fork and tasting the cherry cheesecake. "Oh, that's sooo good. She's smart. She has good solutions to problems."

"She does." Sam had to agree. Why hadn't he just asked her if she could sell them portions? So would she have a solution to his biggest problem?

He motioned her over.

She watched him with what could only be described as neutrality. Apparently, it was too much to expect friendliness.

"We're going to be in the area for a while. Can you recommend a place to stay?"

"Hotel? Bed-and-breakfast? A rental room for a longer stay?"

"Dad needs a job."

Sam choked on a bite of cheesecake and coughed. After a gulp of coffee, he glared at his daughter. No, no, no. This *wasn't* what he'd wanted. He'd planned to glide in under the radar, to get the lay of the land and to see if he could get answers before having to commit to the last, desperate level of subterfuge.

But now it was out in the open. Damn.

"Not really. I—"

"A job? As a ranch hand? Sure," the owner responded almost gleefully. "That can be arranged. There's always room for a hardworking cowboy on any ranch in the county. Especially for an experienced one, which you must be at your age."

Your age? Why was everyone fixated on his age?

Chelsea laughed, enjoying this too much.

"You have your daughter with you," Violet said, "so that will limit the living arrangements. You can't stay in a bunkhouse. Let me see what I can do. I'll make a few calls."

"But—" She left before he could stop her.

"Thanks a lot." He muttered, directing his displeasure toward Chelsea. "Now I can't renege without looking foolish. You shouldn't have mentioned I needed a job. That was supposed to be a last-ditch scenario. I mean *really* last-ditch. I'm not a cowboy."

Chelsea sat back and crossed her arms. He hated her scowl. She used to be sunny and carefree. God, what had he and Tiffany done?

"You shouldn't be dishonest, Dad. You shouldn't be pretending to be someone you're not."

"I don't have a choice."

"Sure you do. Don't you remember what you always used to tell me?"

He blinked. "I've told you a lot of things."

"'Your choices define who you are.'" She mimicked him perfectly at his pedantic worst.

He asked quietly, "Do you really dislike me so much?"

She didn't meet his eyes. Folding and unfolding a corner of her place mat, she mumbled, "No. I don't dislike you."

He believed her. On the other hand, she made sense about the choices he was making here in this town. They weren't his best. But what else could he do? Gramps needed help. The second Gramps had called last week with concerns about the fair, Sam had packed and left. His gramps meant more to him than…than air. More than his father did.

Violet Summer had better be on her game.

A voluptuous figure, violet eyes and thick midnight hair meant nothing. As much as he found the diner owner attractive, he would not be kind to his enemy. Guilty until proved innocent.

Gramps, the greatest guy in Sam's life, deserved to be protected from a bunch of deceitful women.

Chapter Two

"He's conniving and dishonest, Rachel. I'm sure of it," Vy said into the phone in her office. "He's the phoniest cowboy I've ever seen."

"Oh, come on, Vy," her friend responded, "You can't possibly know he's not a real cowboy."

"His boots and hat are spotless. There isn't a speck of dirt or dust on them," Vy said. When that didn't get a response, she added the kicker, "He *irons* his jeans."

"Oh," Rachel breathed into the phone. "I see what you mean." After a pause, she asked, "What do you want from me?"

"You know how you've been complaining about how expensive it's been for Travis to start up his herd?"

Travis Read had moved into town five months ago and had fallen like a ton of bricks for Vy's best friend, Rachel McGuire.

"Setting up the ranch has been a financial challenge," Rachel said. "Especially with his sister no longer moving in and contributing to the mortgage."

Newcomer Sammy Read had found a good match in local rancher Michael Moreno. Her kids needed a father and his children needed a mother. Win-win. Plus, they were super hot for each other.

"No doubt there'll be a wedding soon?"

Rachel laughed. "Like yesterday, if they had their way. As soon as they can organize it." Rachel paused, then said, "Travis has been great with money over the years, but…"

"Getting the ranch going is putting pressure on you?"

"Yeah," Rachel admitted. "But it's the right thing to do. I don't want Travis to have to work for other ranchers for the rest of his life. He wants to be his own boss."

Vy knew how good that felt.

"Plus, his land is beautiful. It would make an excellent ranch. Wouldn't it be amazing for him to have a legacy to leave to both Tori and Beth and any children we might have together?"

"Yeah, it sure would."

Was she doing the right thing in recommending that Travis take on this stranger? She thought so. She'd met evil in her past. She'd known bad men. Her intuition told her this guy wasn't one of them. Besides, she liked his prickly porcupine of a daughter a lot. The girl reminded Vy of herself. On the other hand, there did seem to be something fishy going on with him. What? If it affected her town, Vy needed to know.

Keep your friends close and your enemies closer.

Travis and Rachel were smart people. They could keep an eye on this man.

"Sooo, you and Travis can make extra money by renting the fake cowboy and his daughter the rooms that Sammy and her two boys would have used. What do you think?" When Rachel hesitated, she rushed on, "And Travis would have a ranch hand."

"Not much of one if he's not a real cowboy."

Vy wanted to see the ersatz cowboy brought down.

Unreasonable, Vy. What's your problem? He's done nothing to you, so why the big push to destroy a man you don't even know?

Bits and pieces of memories, of another time and place threatened to intrude, and she turned them aside with a firm resolve.

Nope. She wouldn't be going down that road.

Suffice it to say, she disliked liars.

"Do you think we can trust him in our home?" Rachel asked. A reasonable question.

"Yes. I'm certain he isn't dangerous or I wouldn't have called. Besides, he has his daughter with him. She's either a teenager already or a tween and has some attitude, but don't we all?"

"*You* do," Rachel retorted and Vy laughed.

"True."

"Why are you so upset about this man?" Rachel asked.

Vy didn't want to look too closely at that. She brazened it out. "Anger is my natural response to any kind of charade or dishonesty. I dislike fraud with a passion."

"I know," Rachel said quietly, "but you've never shared why."

Vy sidestepped the deeper issue. "I just don't trust any man who comes to my town with an agenda. If this guy doesn't have a scheme up his sleeve, I'll eat every one of the six coconut-cream pies I made first thing this morning."

She wanted to see him brought down. No! Not true. *She* wanted to bring him down personally.

Too strong a response, Vy. Cool it.

"Tell you what, Vy." Rachel interrupted her thoughts. "We'll give the guy a trial run, but only if you bring out one of those pies this afternoon."

"Deal."

Sam savored the last bite of an exquisite pineapple upside-down cake.

"This is incredible," he said, sighing.

"I know, right?"

"I could eat here every day." He put down his fork and rubbed his stomach. "Take that last bite of chocolate layer cake."

"Are you sure, Dad?"

He smiled. "Honey, don't you know I'd give you my last dollar if it would make you happy?"

For a change, a genuine smile lit Chelsea's face and, while it might be tiny, it reminded him of her smiles of old. And, God, he loved it.

He smiled in return and watched her enjoy the cake.

"Everything's taken care of."

Sam started. The waitress-cum-manager-cum-owner had appeared beside the table without making a sound. He didn't like surprises.

"What do you mean?" he asked, but he knew, and all the good feelings at the table evaporated.

"I called a friend. Her husband's ranch is brand-new. He hasn't hired any hands yet and they could sure use some rent on a couple of spare rooms in the house."

She slapped a paper with directions on it onto the table and picked up the cash he'd left for their meal.

Sam was trapped.

He'd left New York too quickly and without enough preparation. He *hated* this feeling.

But how could he leave without solving Gramps's dilemma first?

He needed to blend in. He'd done research online. Successful no matter what he took on, he could do this.

But damn, he didn't know a thing about working on a ranch. He'd be as naive as Chelsea if he thought he could be any good as a cowboy after one night of research. This had been a crazy idea from the start.

Sam opened his mouth to object, to halt this mad process before it went too far, but Violet raised her hand.

"No need to thank me. It's what people around here do. Help each other out." An odd smile hovered at the edges of her full red lips, as though she were having a laugh at his expense, reminding him of his daughter's smiles these days. "Travis is a newcomer himself, so he'll make you feel welcome. His wife, Rachel, will take good care of Chelsea while you're working. Or will she be enrolling in the local school?"

"Not yet," Sam replied, not expanding on the subject. No need to air dirty laundry here.

Sam wondered why Chelsea didn't object to having a babysitter, this woman Rachel, before realizing his child enjoyed his discomfort. She knew he was trapped.

Gramps. Think of Gramps. This is all for him.

"Sure," he said weakly. "Sounds good."

"By the way, in case you didn't realize, I'm Violet Summer."

He figured as much, and Rachel's last name must be McGuire, one of the women Gramps had told him about. Before his time in this town ended, he'd meet all six of the women resurrecting the fair and possibly ripping off his grandfather.

"I'm Sam—" He'd almost said Carmichael. He'd been christened Carson Samuel Carmichael like his father and grandfather, but his mother had always called him Sam to distinguish him from his father. That part was easy, but changing Carmichael to Michaels had nearly caught him up. "I'm Sam Michaels. This is my daughter, Chelsea."

"I'm sure I'll be seeing you around town."

He had to start *thinking* of himself as Sam Michaels or he'd never pull this off.

Chelsea shot him a look of censure at his name change but he ignored her.

Sam picked up his hat on the way out of the diner, stepping onto Rodeo's Main Street and standing a minute to look around town. Might as well know what he was getting into.

So this was his father's hometown, the one Dad had left at nineteen when he'd headed east to attend college. He'd made, and married into, a lot of money in New York City. Carson II had never returned to Rodeo, which meant that Sam himself had never been here, either.

Sam craned his neck to take it all in, curious about his dad's town. Dad had never talked much about Rodeo, but Gramps sure had.

Rodeo, Montana. Gramps's favorite spot on earth.

He'd described everything to the avid little listener Sam had been as a boy. Two stoplights on Main Street and one small shop after another with names like Jorgenson's Hardware and Hiram's Pharmacy and Nelly's Dos 'n' Don'ts.

Angled parking ran all along a wide street filled with plenty of pickup trucks heavy with rust, dust and dirt.

He drank in every detail, his avidity surprising him with its intensity. He hadn't realized until arriving how much he'd wanted to see Gramps's town.

Why hadn't Dad ever talked about Rodeo? It didn't look so bad. Just the opposite in fact, charming but real, unpretentious and normal compared to Manhattan, where people seemed compelled to jump on every trend.

In this town, every man, woman and child wore well-used denim. Sam detected not a single pair of designer jeans.

Thank God the jeans he'd bought before they left home were plain and would fit in. He'd gone to a work-wear clothing store to find denim without embroidered pockets or slashed knees or distress wash thighs or fake-faded creases or any of the other fads going around.

Certain he fit in, he adjusted his cowboy hat. Here, almost everyone wore a cowboy hat.

Sam soaked it all up like the proverbial sponge. Gramps hadn't lied about his good-looking, if rustic, town.

And Sam was immediately smitten.

"What are you doing, Dad?"

"Savoring the heritage I've never checked out until now."

"Why didn't you ever check it out?"

"School and then work and then getting married and then having you. You know…" He shrugged. "Life."

"Let's go to the car," Chelsea demanded. Back to doom, gloom and *'tude*, as Violet had called it, all traces of the friendly girl who'd laughed with the waitress dissipated on the cool air.

Sam grimaced. When he'd married Tiffany, he'd believed in "for better or for worse." Apparently, she hadn't.

He'd loved her. Not so much since her betrayal, though.

He felt the same way about children. You loved them. You did not give up on them. Purely and simply, they deserved to be loved through thick and thin, without question. He just wished right now that it were easier, especially when he had so much on his mind.

"Let's go visit Gramps," he said.

Chelsea ran to their vehicle. "Come on, Dad. Don't be so slow."

Ah, enthusiasm. She did love her grandfather. Until recently, he'd come to Manhattan for Christmas every year, but now lived in a retirement home.

"We should have come here sooner to visit Gramps."

Yep. Love for her grandfather for sure.

Correction, *his* grandfather, but they'd dispensed with

the *great* part of great-grandfather when Chelsea was little and it had proved too much of a mouthful for her. To Chelsea, he was just Gramps, exactly as he was for Sam.

An old cowboy nodded to him and Sam smiled and nodded back. Friendly people.

They drove toward the next small town, where a seniors' residence that served the entire county housed Sam's nearest and dearest. They passed spectacular scenery on the way.

Chelsea shouted, "Dad, look!"

Sam glanced to his right. In the field a pair of young lambs ran up one side of a small hillock and down the other, kicking up their heels at the top.

"Frisky," he commented.

"So cute." In her voice, he heard longing and wonder, refreshing to hear after her recent negativity. His daughter loved animals.

"Remember when you saw all of those baby lambs at that petting zoo and we couldn't drag you away for an hour? You were only six years old and fascinated."

Good memories.

She smiled. "That was awesome. You convinced them to let me sit on some hay and hold one for, like, an hour."

Sam squeezed her hand. "It was only fifteen minutes, but you were small and that was a long time for you. I think I took twenty photographs. You were so cute."

"It was the *best*, but it's even better to see them out frolicking in their natural habitat, isn't it?"

"It sure is." He slowed down. "Do you want to watch for a while?"

"Can we?" She sounded so hopeful he couldn't disappoint her.

He sat on the shoulder for fifteen minutes listening to Chelsea laugh, the sound a sweet balm for his ravaged psyche. For the past year and a half, he'd missed his ex-wife's presence in his life, but even more, he'd missed his daughter's laughter. He wanted to make her happy again.

"I guess we should go," he said reluctantly.

Sounding contented, she said, "Yeah. I want to see Gramps."

A couple of miles later, Sam pulled onto the shoulder of the small highway with a squeal of brakes and spraying gravel.

"Dad, what are you doing?"

"Look."

He pointed across the road.

"What's that?" Chelsea asked.

"That, my dear child, is your heritage."

"That's Gramps's amusement park?"

He heard the doubt in her voice. It echoed in his chest.

Gramps might have raved about his fairgrounds during his visits, but it looked bad. Most of the rides were rusty. A few were in the process of being updated and fixed. One was being dismantled by a couple of old men with a pair of tractors.

Far off to the right and back from the road a fair distance was Gramps's house but Gramps was no longer there.

Sam had never seen the house but he recognized it from his grandfather's descriptions and old photographs. Some of those had been black-and-white, shot in the days when the fairgrounds were brand-new more than a century ago, and built by Gramps's father.

A tidal wave of emotion swept through him, longing, need and anger culminating in one word: *mine*.

He owned a beautiful apartment in the city overlooking Central Park and a huge home in upstate New York. So why should a plain two-story brick home with tilting front steps affect him so? With its modest proportions, two windows on the first floor and three above, the ordinary house didn't compare well to the showstopper he owned with ten spacious bedrooms. This one had, what? Three? Four, maybe?

Yet he wanted it.

That house, these fairgrounds, leased now to a bunch of locals intent on making a profit from his grandfather's belongings, were out of Sam's reach.

An old saying or song lyric, Sam couldn't remember which, thrummed through him. *You don't know what you've got till it's gone.* Wasn't that the truth?

Throughout the busy years, thoughts of Rodeo had been stored in a far corner of his mind, taken out only at Christmas when Gramps came to visit. In all of those years, he had thought the town, and the fairgrounds, would be here waiting for him.

Then his life had changed. Drastically.

Last year, it had taken a crazy turn. Now he was about to start a new business in New York.

Success is the best revenge.

The idea consumed him. Even so, a part of him yearned for the house, toward knowing and understanding his rural heritage.

But, for the short time he would be here, he wouldn't be able to get to know it.

At least for the next year, those women had control of Sam's heritage. Worse, Gramps couldn't remember how long he'd agreed to make the lease. What if it was two, three, five years before Sam got it back?

"Dad, isn't it beautiful?" Chelsea's voice whispered out on a breathy sigh. "It's awesome."

The fairgrounds? Maybe after a massive amount of work. But now? Awesome? No.

She pointed to something and his eyes adjusted focus

from the distant house to the foreground, to a ride right in front of him—a carousel that had been rejuvenated with colorful paint.

Chelsea was right. *Awesome* was a good word for it, all fresh and spit shined. Did the machine work? Were the women planning to give rides on it?

If so, it looked like Chelsea might be first in line.

Hope and potential all rolled into one, it stood in the weak March sunlight proudly declaring "If I can be saved, so can the rest of this old place."

A powerful sentiment.

"It's got really weird animals," Chelsea said, but he detected no disdain.

"You're right. Is that a bull?"

"Yeah, and a couple of sheep."

"Bighorn sheep, I'm pretty sure."

"There's a bison! And a cow." She giggled, the sound sweet on the cool breeze. "What are those?"

"An elk and two white-tailed deer."

"Their saddles are so beautiful. So ornate. I want to ride all of them." She peered up at him. "Will we still be here when the fair is on?"

Apparently, they planned to launch in August and it was only March. Sam's next business venture started in one month. He had only thirty days to get this problem sorted out so he could hightail it home.

No way was he losing out on the opportunity to make serious money with his new investment firm, Carmichael, Jones and Raven. Between the three partners, their experience totaled fifty years. Sam planned to take the industry by storm.

If, along the way, he showed up his ex-wife and father-in-law and the company they'd wrestled away from him during the divorce, all the better. Answering Chelsea's question about attending the fair, he said, "It isn't likely, possum."

His nickname for his daughter slipped out before thought or caution. For some reason, as a little girl, Chelsea had taken a liking to Dame Edna and had giggled every time *possum* was used as an endearment.

Sam had called her possum once and she'd rolled on the floor laughing. The name had stuck.

Sometimes at night, he could hear her accessing YouTube on her laptop and watching old shows she must know by heart.

Entranced by the carousel, she didn't call him to task for the nickname she, these days, called stupid.

"I don't know what's going to happen here."

"If you have your way, there won't even be a fair." How could one young girl hold so much bitterness? Had the divorce harmed her beyond repair?

He hoped not, with a fierceness that shocked him.

"You know what? This place looks bad now, but I can see the potential. I can see what Gramps and his father built."

Chelsea nodded. "Yeah, it must have been really cool years ago."

"I agree." Dad must have spent a fair bit of time every summer working here. Then he'd walked away from it all and never looked back.

Sam couldn't get enough of the place. He could stand here for hours checking it out. Even better, he'd like to walk the land. It might be derelict now, but it must have been magical in its day.

"I should ask Gramps if I can get in to look around."

"Can I come, too?"

"Of course."

Sighing, he straightened away from the fence.

"Let's go visit Gramps and then find this ranch I'm supposed to be working on."

Chelsea snorted. He ignored it. It had been a long trip. He'd had plenty of practice ignoring her.

On second thought...

He pulled out the change purse, opened it and held it out to her. "Snorting."

"It's not really snorting, Dad," she said in her best disdainful teenage voice. "Nobody really snorts."

Sam imitated a pig by letting out a huge snort. Chelsea tried not to giggle.

"I don't walk around sounding like a pig. It's more like humphing."

"I know, but it has the same effect. Lack of respect. Pay up."

She snorted again, rummaged in her pocket and came up with a quarter.

Chapter Three

At the seniors' residence, Sam parked and they got out of the car.

Sam had come to Rodeo to check out this place along with the women.

Gramps had been admitted nine or so months ago, when much of Sam's life had still been in a state of flux, with visits to the lawyer's office almost a daily occurrence.

Sam had seen many horror stories about elder abuse on the news. He hadn't known what to expect, but the two-story residence looked homey. Wide windows on the first floor looked out on golden fields and gray mountains in the distance.

"This doesn't look so bad," Sam said.

Sam corresponded with Gramps regularly, but hadn't seen him in a couple of years thanks to his messy divorce. Whatever had been happening in his own life, he should have taken the time to come see his grandfather, to make sure everything was okay.

Considering that Gramps had visited every year since Sam was born, his canceled trips had been a real cause for concern.

Then again, he was pushing ninety.

At the reception desk, they got his room number. Sam

found the pace of his steps quickening the farther down the hallway he strode and the closer he got to his grandfather.

As a child, Sam's life with Mom and Dad had been formal and less than affectionate. But Gramps had been all about hugs, kisses and effusive expressions of love. Sweet balm to a lonely kid.

They rounded the corner into his room and Chelsea bounded over to the frail man in the wheelchair beside the window.

"Chelsea! Sam!" Gramps clung to his great-granddaughter with closed eyes. When he opened them, they were watery.

"You've grown." His voice, anything but frail, jumped with love and his irreverent humor. "You're a young woman. What's all of this?"

He studied the black nail polish. He feathered a touch over the spider's web of mascara obscuring her pretty blue eyes.

"Where did all of this come from? Where's my little Chelsea?"

Chelsea shoved her hands behind her back. She shrugged, moody again.

Gramps touched her cheek and smiled. "You're still my beautiful girl."

He turned his gimlet gaze on Sam. "What's with the hat and boots? You've never worn cowboy boots in your life."

Sam surged forward to shake his hand. Still surprisingly strong, Gramps pulled him down for a hug. Sam hung on, love rushing through him like a clear mountain stream. His vision misted.

"It's good to see you," Sam said and then cleared his throat. When he straightened, he kept his grandfather's hand clutched in his own.

This, *this*, was why he was here, to protect this dear old guy. Heaven help this town if they cheated his grandfather.

Gramps's eyes were damp again, too. They'd struck up this magical bond through the annual visits Gramps had made to New York City.

When finally old enough to understand how much Gramps hated the city, Sam realized the sacrifice Gramps made in spending every Christmas with Sam instead of in his beloved town.

His love for his only grandchild was clear.

It served to cement Sam's love for him all the more.

"We're here incognito, Gramps," Chelsea blurted. Sam wished she hadn't. He'd planned to ease into the particular form of subterfuge he'd originally hoped he wouldn't have to use.

Gramps came to attention. "You're here to fix my problem?"

"Yes. I told you I was coming to help."

"Yeah, but what's this about being incognito?" Gramps frowned. "What does Chelsea mean?"

No help for it now. He might as well jump in.

"She's right," Sam admitted. "I'm not using Carmichael. We're here as the Michaelses. We're Sam and Chelsea Michaels."

"Why?" Gramps sounded frail.

"To find out exactly what's going on with the fair those women in town are putting on this summer."

"I asked you to make sure they aren't cheating me. I thought you would come here to confront them directly."

"I decided this was better."

"You want to be dishonest."

"Not *want*. I *need* to be dishonest to catch these women in *their* dishonesty."

"But I thought—why can't you just be yourself?"

"That's what I asked, too."

"Chelsea, for once can you support your dad? I'm not

the villain here. Gramps, you leased the land to them for only one dollar. Now you can't remember how long the lease stands. You didn't get a written contract out of them. I have nothing to read over, nothing to verify what the deal is. We know nothing about how the profits will be split. I find it shameful that these people only offered you a dollar."

Sam scrubbed his hands over his face. "You asked me to find out if they're ripping you off. *This* is how I'm doing it."

He pointed to both Gramps and Chelsea. "Neither of you gets to decide how it should be done. I'm helping out in my own way. Period."

"But—"

Ire roused, Sam asked, "Do you think if I asked if they were being honest with you that I'd get a straight response? Come on. That's naive. I've worked in business for close to twenty years. I know how important it is to protect oneself with a written contract. How do you know this revival committee won't rob you blind if I don't come in under the radar to find out?"

"I know. I know." Gramps raised a placating hand. "It's just—I've known most of 'em since they were in diapers. I thought I trusted them, but…" Gramps looked lost. "I don't know what's wrong. I don't know what to do."

He sounded so plaintive, so unlike the strong, vibrant man Sam had always known. Beside him, Chelsea made a small sound that might have been distress.

"You don't have to do anything, Gramps," Sam said. "That's why I'm here." He squeezed his grandfather's shoulder. "So you don't know exactly what I should look for?"

"No. All I have is a feeling." Gramps turned from staring out the window to pin him with a glare. "You just got divorced. Is your ex bleeding you dry? Why are you helping me? Are you afraid of losing your inheritance?"

The change in tone and subject sent Sam reeling.

"No!" What had ever given Gramps the idea that Sam wanted him to die so he could have his money? Gramps had never spoken to him with this harsh a tone before. "How can you think that? I want you to live forever. This isn't about me. It's about protecting *you*."

Gramps relaxed back into his chair, momentarily bewildered. That confusion worried Sam. Gramps had always been sharp.

He shared a worried frown with Chelsea.

Gramps puckered his forehead. "If it's not about your inheritance, why are you so worried?"

"Because *you* are. You put your life into that place and only left when your body was no longer up to the work."

"Yeah? So?"

"So, I know how much it meant to you. When you retired, I thought it would live on in everyone's memories as *your* tradition carried down from your father."

"Uh-huh. So?"

"So…these women are stealing your history and your legacy."

"That's what you're worried about? I thought it was money."

"Of course I'm worried about money. They're giving you one dollar for use of the land with no contract for a percentage of the profits."

When Gramps didn't respond, Sam asked, "You are getting *some* of the profits, aren't you?"

Gramps's gaze slid away before admitting, "I don't remember."

Sam swore under his breath, worry burrowing into him. Gramps wasn't the type to forget this kind of thing.

"I got an idea, though, about what's going on." Gramps smiled. "With you, I mean."

"With me? How is any of this about me? There's nothing going on with me."

"Sure there is. You're going on about history and legacy and tradition. None of that going to matter to me when I'm gone. You're worried about heritage for *your* sake. Not mine."

Stunned, Sam stared. "No... I..."

"It's true. I remember how you used to listen to all my stories. Now that you're finally here, because of this revival, you won't be able to have any part of it like you'd thought you would some day."

"But—" Hard to argue with the truth. Today, seeing the amusement park for the first time and Gramps's house and Gramps, yeah, he did care about his heritage. "I care about them ripping you off, too."

"The money. Yeah. But I don't know if I'm being ripped off."

"But you didn't sign anything."

"Nope. Not a single sheet of paper."

"So even if you had negotiated for a share of the profits, you have no idea what you agreed to. So these women could make up any terms they want."

Gramps's brow furrowed. Then he perked up and a wide grin split his old face. "They won't hurt me, Sam. Ever."

Sam stopped pacing. Gramps's behavior worried him. Confused at one moment and happy the next. Distrustful and then immediately certain the women meant him no harm. Sensing mental deterioration, Sam needed to talk to his grandfather's doctor. How could Gramps forget the details about the deal he'd made with the women?

"I can't believe that remark about the inheritance."

A twinkle in Gramps's eye mollified him. "After all

you've been through lately, it's a relief you're still my great, honorable grandson."

"What's honorable about pretending to be someone he isn't?" Chelsea asked.

"His heart's in the right place," Gramps replied. "That's all I need to know."

Time to move forward on everything. "Okay, let's go over their names. We've already met one of them. The diner owner."

"Violet Summer," Gramps said.

"We stopped there for lunch. I can't say she left a good impression. She's opinionated and sarcastic."

Chelsea giggled. "She didn't like the way Dad flirted with her." She did her impression of him complimenting Violet's eyes.

Gramps barked out a laugh. "Nope. Vy wouldn't like that. She doesn't suffer fools gladly."

"I'm not a fool."

"No, you aren't, Sam, but Vy doesn't know you yet."

Eager to move off the topic of the diner owner with curves in all the right places, Sam said, "Chelsea and I are going to be staying with another of the women. Rachel McGuire."

"Yep, she lives now with her husband, Travis Read. What do you mean, you'll be staying with them?"

Sam explained about getting a job on the new ranch.

"A job?" Gramps picked up a cup from a small table and took a sip from a straw. "Doing what?"

"He's going to be a cowboy, Gramps." *When* had she become such a tattletale?

Orange juice sprayed from Gramps's mouth and down the front of his shirt. Sam expected embarrassment or at the very least dismay, but Gramps laughed hard.

Chelsea giggled with him.

Sam blotted OJ from Gramps's shirt.

When he finally stopped laughing, Gramps gasped. "What do you know about being a cowboy?"

Sam stiffened. "Enough to get by." Not really, but he wouldn't admit it. His pride was taking a beating in this town.

"There is no *getting by* in ranching. It's hard work. You either know what you're doing or you don't. Where'd you learn about it? On your computer?"

Because that is exactly what he'd done, Sam didn't respond.

"Dear Lord, I'm right, aren't I? You looked at some pictures on the line—"

"Online, Gramps," Chelsea said and Sam wanted to object. *Don't encourage him*.

"And maybe read, what, a couple of books or magazines? Now you think you know how it's done?"

Still, Sam didn't respond. He wasn't as naive as they thought. He knew he'd be faking *a lot*, but he was doing the best he could with the little he had.

"My God, don't do this." Gramps slammed his juice cup onto the table. "It shows disrespect for real cowboys. They aren't some cliché you see in old movies. They're real hard workers. I admire those men and women. They are as tough as they come but can be real gentle when they need to be."

"What do you mean, Gramps?" Sam's daughter, who didn't care about anything Sam said these days, hung on her great-grandfather's every word.

"They love their animals, but will put one down in the blink of an eye if it's in pain. Tough people."

"Put one down?" Chelsea squeaked.

"Yep, sweetheart. If they have to."

"Even their own, like, horses?"

"Or dogs. Knew a kid, only thirteen, out plowing in the field. Ran over his dog. No one else was home. Dog was mangled, suffering something fierce, dying. That boy ran to the house and loaded a rifle. When he got back to his dog, he shot him. Put him out of his misery."

Chelsea covered her mouth with her black-nailed hands. "He killed his own dog? Gramps, that's awful."

"Yeah, but it was the right thing to do. Showed compassion. Said it was the toughest thing he'd ever done in his life. 'Course, his life isn't over yet. Who knows what else he'll be called on to do before his life is over."

Chelsea stared at Sam, the look in her eye clearly saying, "Could you do that?"

Chelsea and Gramps didn't get that he could be as tough as he needed to be to protect his family.

Sam knew how hard the job would be, but he also knew he was strong. Maybe not in the same way but durable enough in spirit. He'd be damned before he let anyone in this town get the better of his grandfather.

"You think you can take on that kind of job?" Gramps watched him.

"I will do the job to the best of my abilities. I'm a hard worker, I don't mind putting in long hours and I'm more capable than you think."

Gramps's expression softened. "Your parents were quick to share your accomplishments. They were always proud. I know how smart you are and all the things you've done, but this is another barrel of horseshoes altogether."

Sam needed to steer away from this argument.

"Who are the other women? I forget their names." He didn't really. Sam had a mind like a steel trap, but he hoped Gramps might have some new information to help Sam get the job done.

"Nadine Campbell, Honey Armstrong and Max Porter. Oh, and a new one. Samantha Read."

"Any relation to the guy, Travis, who we're heading off to meet?"

"His sister," Gramps responded. "New to town like him."

"If these women are so keen to do something for this town, why don't they create something of their own instead of taking over your fair and rodeo?"

"Because the fair is there and already set up. The rides, the concession stands, the fairgrounds, the barns and stables. All they have to do is renovate and update." His grandfather stared out of the window again. "I never wanted it to lie fallow all of those years. It's special, Sam."

Before Sam could say anything, his grandfather glanced from his grandchild to his great-grandchild. "Go see the fairgrounds. It's your heritage. Take Chelsea. It's her heritage, too."

"We did, Gramps," Chelsea said. "I love it."

"You saw it?"

"On the way over here."

A slow smile spread on Gramps's face. "You love it?"

"Yeah. It's magical."

"It sure is," Gramps agreed.

The two of them talked like children, Gramps taking a childlike delight in Chelsea's enthusiasm. While pleased to see him happy, Sam had to remember to bring it up with Gramps's doctor. Was it regression?

To Sam, he said, "I never agreed with your father's decision not to bring you home to visit."

Sam didn't like criticism of his parents, even if their values didn't always jibe with his own.

"Don't grimace, Sam. This should have been as much

your home as New York was. It's your heritage. And now you can finally get to know the place and the people."

"Why didn't Dad ever come home? He would never tell me when I asked."

"A woman," Gramps barked. "Why else? He was young and foolish and heartbroken. Silly pup."

"Who? Did the woman stay in town?"

"She married someone else. She's still here."

"Dad did all right with Mom. They seemed to be happy." His mom had died five years ago.

Gramps motioned for Sam to come around to the back of his chair. "Push me out to the sunroom. Faces east. Too hot in the morning. Have to wait until afternoon. It'll be cool enough now."

Sam wheeled him down the hallway, with Chelsea walking alongside holding Gramps's hand. "Which way?"

"Right at the far end." He took a big plaid hankie out of his pocket and blew his nose. "Pretending to be a cowboy might be your first failure, Sam."

No, not his first. Not even close.

What of his marriage? What of his wife leaving in the most dishonest way possible? What of not protecting himself from his father-in-law?

What of not being able to protect his child from the fallout?

He glanced at Chelsea. What of his failure to bridge the gap that separated them?

Sam positioned Gramps beside a window that looked out onto a golden field with low purple-gray hills in the distance.

"Can you visit while you're staying in Rodeo or will that blow your cover?"

Blow his cover? "Gramps, this isn't a spy movie. But, yeah, we'll visit a lot. Wild horses couldn't keep me away."

Or maybe they would. Were cowboys still expected to break in Mustangs? He didn't have a clue. He'd have to look it up online. Why? No way could he fake *that*.

Could he fake any of it?

In the solarium, another resident, a tiny woman with an eye for Gramps and a tiny shih tzu in her lap caught Chelsea's attention, and she went and played with the dog and talked to the woman.

Yet again, she had more smiles for everyone else than she did for him. A split second of despair rattled him. How did he bridge the gap?

"She sure likes animals, doesn't she?" Gramps asked.

"She's never met an animal she didn't like."

"How long you planning to stay?"

"I have a month to determine the intentions of these women."

"How come you can take so much time off work? I know you're the owner of the company, but shouldn't you be there to oversee things?"

For a few tense moments, Sam worried in silence. He'd already explained all of this on the phone to Gramps before he came. "I no longer own the company. Tiffany got it as part of the divorce settlement. She bought me out. To be accurate, her father bought me out. Since he'd bankrolled the company for Tiff and me at the start and owned a controlling share, it was easy for him to pull the rug out from under me."

The betrayal had come on so many levels. "Those two. That snake." Aching with all he had to say, he nonetheless held back with Chelsea nearby. After all, Tiffany's father was her grandfather.

Sam leaned against the wall. "I'm free for the next month." He knew he sounded bitter. Divorce and losing his livelihood, even if he had come out ahead with millions in the bank, had never been part of his life's plan. He told his grandfather about the new venture starting in a month.

"You sound excited."

"I am, Gramps. I don't like to be idle." In fact, without the formation of the new firm, Sam didn't know what he would do with his life. He'd never, not once, felt so rudderless.

Even these months off since the company had been given over to Tiffany had been hell.

He felt better when he had purpose and activity driving his days. As well, there were those thoughts ringing through him, every day, about success and revenge.

Oh, yeah, he'd like to show Tiffany and her father how successful he could be without them. And he would. Be successful, that was.

He had a talent for business. Not so with this cowboy stuff. What had he been thinking?

"Always felt the same way myself," Gramps said. "Didn't want to be idle for a single second of the day." They visited for an hour while Sam itched to get to the ranch, to find out how hard his job was going to be and whether he was truly up to the task.

On the way out, he stopped at the nurse's desk and asked about Gramps's doctor. He wouldn't be in until Monday. Sam would have to wait for answers.

As soon as they left the building, Chelsea voiced what she'd obviously been thinking inside.

"Dad, I'm worried."

"About Gramps? Me, too. He's not himself."

They got into the SUV and drove away.

"Dad…"

Sam glanced away from the road for a second. Chelsea chewed on her bottom lip.

"What is it, possum? Something worrying you? Spit it out."

"You've been strange lately. Is it because of the divorce?"

"Strange how?"

He sensed her shrugging beside him. "I don't know. More hard. Tougher. You were an easygoing guy and so much fun. I loved that about you. But now you don't seem to like people anymore. You don't trust anyone."

"Yeah. True. That's because of the divorce." Sam hesitated to criticize Tiffany to her daughter. "I'm not comfortable talking to you about your mother behind her back, but her…"

"Her affair, Dad. I know what she did. She shouldn't have slept with that guy."

Sam hated that Chelsea knew about that kind of thing. "Her betrayal was profound," he admitted. "It's going to take a long time for me to trust like I used to."

The farther they drove away from Gramps and the closer they got to the ranch, the more Chelsea slumped in her seat. She crossed her arms and settled into the sulk she'd been in for the drive out.

Gone were the smiles for Gramps and the old woman with her cute dog.

"I don't want to stay with people we don't know. I wish Gramps wasn't in an old-folks' home so we could stay with him."

"You and me both, Chelsea." He thought of the two-story house that sat on Gramps's land. Tonight, they could have been sleeping in the very house his dad had grown up in if the townsfolk hadn't talked Gramps out of his land.

ONCE THE LUNCH crowd finally left and she knew she had a couple of hours before launching dinner service, Violet packaged up a container of rice pudding for her friend Rachel and Rachel's daughter, Tori. They both loved it. She added a jar of parsnip soup for Travis.

At the last minute, she remembered the coconut-cream pie Rachel had bargained for.

Why was the new man in town pretending to be a cowboy? Did he think people in Rodeo were so stupid they wouldn't notice? Who was he? Why was he here?

Since he'd left her diner, questions hadn't stopped swirling through Vy's brain.

Rodeo had taken her in with open arms fourteen years ago as a grieving sixteen-year-old and she'd spent her years here giving back ever since.

This close to resurrecting the fair and rodeo that would bring much-needed tourism dollars to the town, they couldn't take a chance on anything going wrong.

What could that project possibly have to do with the new stranger in town, Vy?

She had no idea.

She phoned Rachel. "Is he there yet?"

"Not yet, Vy."

"Why not, I wonder? Why didn't he go straight to the ranch? If he isn't there, where is he?"

"Why are you so worried about him?"

Vy bit her bottom lip. "Maybe I'm seeing shadows where there aren't any, but what if he tries to screw up the fair and rodeo somehow?"

"Vy, that's a *huge* leap. Why would this guy have anything to do with our fair?"

"He has money. I'm sure of it. Maybe he wants to steal our ideas and put on his own show."

"That's crazy talk. You're overreacting. What's gotten into you? You usually have more common sense than this."

"I just… God, Rachel, I don't know." She sighed, battered by intuition not based in fact and clueless about her worry. She tried to shrug it off. Strangers came through all the time, for Pete's sake. "I'm coming over for a visit, anyway. I've got food."

Rachel laughed. "Yum. Good. I'm exhausted. Beth was up nursing every two hours last night. Must be a growth spurt."

"Plenty of tasty calories on the way to replace what that little cutie is using up."

Vy loaded the food into her car and drove out of town.

She slowed down when she realized the SUV she followed on the small rural highway possibly belonged to the stranger. Okay, so she hadn't been above watching him leave the diner to check out his vehicle. Good thing. She didn't want to walk in at the same time.

She pulled onto the shoulder to sit and allow Sam and his daughter to get inside the house.

Travis Read had bought the Victorian on the two-lane highway when he'd moved to town back in October or November.

In the past, he'd been determined to remain single and not be tied down. But he'd quickly fallen for Rodeo's own effervescent, lovely Rachel—even though she'd already had a three-year-old and had been more than seven months pregnant with her second.

In the end, he'd taken on a ready-made family, a house and a new ranch.

Vy glanced across the road toward the ratty trailer from which he'd rescued Rachel. Dark and lonesome against the cloudy sky, it stood like a festering wound.

Trailers left Vy feeling antsy and slightly nauseated. She hated them. Hated what they represented to her.

Despite her envy, she was damned glad Rachel and her children had a real home now.

Vy didn't need a husband and children. Men were a complication she avoided outside the odd booty call with one of the town's more reliable, discreet single guys.

What else could she possibly need from a man?

She loved her independence. Enough said.

SAM STEPPED OUT of the car in front of the big old Victorian and wondered why the owner of the diner ever thought to call this a ranch.

All along the highway, he'd passed low-slung ranch houses better suited to the prairie. But he could probably take the house and plunk it down into an old Boston neighborhood. He fully expected to find a parlor inside outfitted with velvet sofas and crocheted doilies.

After knocking on the oak door, he waited, his stomach dancing with nerves. How did he possibly think he could handle this?

He *could* handle it. Look how well he'd done with the Harper acquisition. He'd made millions on that. Or how he'd managed to fight off the hostile takeover by Steig Industries.

He could do just about anything. As long as they didn't have him shoveling manure, he should be fine.

Well, duh. Of course, cowboys shovel manure. Chelsea's imagined sarcasm sounded in his head.

She sat in the car, elbow deep in a self-indulgent pout.

The door opened before Sam raised his hand to knock again.

A tall, fair-haired man stood in the dim hallway, denim shirt and pants outlining a work-hardened body. A chiseled jaw and enough fine lines at the corners of his blue eyes to add character prevented a slide into movie-star territory.

"I'm Travis Read." He stuck out his hand. "You must

be Sam. Rachel told me you were coming. Expected you sooner."

"I drove around a bit. I've never been in Montana before. It's beautiful." Not a complete lie. He and Chelsea had seen a bit of the country on their way to the nursing home and here.

"Come on in." Travis peered beyond Sam and asked, "Is that your daughter in the car? Doesn't she want to come inside?"

"She's…she's not completely happy we're here." He left it at that.

A tiny girl, only three or so, popped up beside Travis. "You gots a little girl? I go get her."

"She's not little," Sam began, but the girl shot off the veranda and tried to open the car door.

Sam reached her and opened the passenger door. Maybe this cute child would succeed where Sam hadn't. Her dimples could charm even a hardened criminal.

"Hi," she said to Chelsea, leaning into the car. "My name's Victoria. Mommy calls me Tori. What's your name?" Without waiting for a reply, she forged on. "I gots pink cowboy boots. Look! Do you gots cowboy boots? Why don't you come out? We can play."

Chelsea glanced at Sam helplessly and he understood why. As much as Chelsea adored animals, she loved children even more. Hard to hold on to a good pout when a charming little girl asked you to come out to play.

He waited with a smile on his lips. Any second now, Chelsea had to give in to the girl's charm.

"Is your seat belt stuck?" Tori asked. "You can't get it off? I hep you!"

Tori climbed up onto Chelsea to reach the seat belt connection. Chelsea said "Oof" and laughed.

"It's okay, Tori, I can do it. I'll get out now."

Tori climbed back out with Chelsea's supporting hand on her back so she wouldn't fall. Chelsea unsnapped her seat belt and left the car.

Tori grabbed her hand and pulled her toward the house.

"Does anyone ever say no to that child?" Sam asked.

Travis grinned. "No one I've met yet."

Sam followed him, Chelsea and Tori into the house.

He'd been wrong about the interior. Completely. No sedate, old-fashioned Victorian, sage-green living room walls contrasted the solid oak floor and the dark wood trim nicely. A huge fireplace dominated one side of the room.

On the walls, several large landscapes startled with their colors and subject matter, at once roughhewn and refined, powerful and elegant. Painted by the same hand as the ones in the diner?

Travis caught him studying them. "Local artist. Zachary Brandt."

"Local scenery?"

Travis nodded.

"Beautiful."

"Sit, please. I'll get Rachel. Let's get to know each other before you start work."

Work. Sam swallowed. What exactly would it entail here?

Rachel, an attractive woman with a warm smile and a baby in her arms, joined them, and after introductions and glasses of fresh lemonade were produced, they all sat.

Sam struggled with how to break the ice, but Tori took care of that. She lounged against Travis's leg with her little feet crossed at the ankle and rested one elbow on Travis's knee and her chin on her hand.

She directed all of her attention toward Chelsea.

"You gots nail polish. You like black. I like your hair. Is it soft?"

Chelsea nodded.

"Can I feel it?"

Chelsea nodded again.

Tori approached and touched it. "Oh, it's so soft. Pretty."
Now she leaned on Chelsea's knee.

"Travis is gonna buy me a pony. Do you gots a pony?"
Chelsea nodded.

Tori's eyes widened. "Mommy! Travis! Chels gots a pony!"

Sam smiled at the girl's attempt to pronounce his daughter's name.

Tori leaned close to Chelsea. "What's his name?"

Chelsea's cheeks turned suspiciously pink. Sam knew
why. He waited and watched, the corner of his mouth kicking up into a smug smile. She'd been making fun of him for
close to two thousand miles. Nice to have the tables turned.

"Zayn," Chelsea mumbled.

Tori wrinkled her tiny nose. "That's a funny name. Why
did you named him that?"

Chelsea mumbled again but no one heard her reply.

"Speak up, Chelsea," Sam urged. "Tell them why you
chose Zayn."

"Daaad."

"Inquiring minds want to know."

Despite her mutinous expression, she admitted, "After
Zayn Malik, who used to be in One Direction. Okay?"

Tori, sensing Chelsea's embarrassment, patted her knee.
"It's okay. It's a nice name. Is he cute?"

"He's *so* cute," Chelsea breathed. "He's got the darkest
eyes. Like melted chocolate. You can just sink into them
and get lost."

Sam grinned. "She means the pony, Chelsea."

His daughter's cheeks darkened further.

Chelsea ignored him and told Tori, "He's a super cute
pony. The prettiest one of all of my friends'."

"Where is he?"

"In New—"

"He's stabled with a friend," Sam cut in, sending Chelsea a warning plea. *Don't blow my cover*, to use Gramps's term. "It's only until we decide where we're going to live in Montana. My horse is at home, too. Do you have a spare one I can use?"

If Sam had let Chelsea finish saying New York, would Travis wonder how Sam could possibly be a real cowboy having just come from the east? So many layers of dishonesty...

He might have held his cards close to his chest in business, but he'd never been a liar.

Chelsea crossed her arms and pouted again.

Rachel and Travis exchanged glances but, thank God, didn't ask for clarification.

"I can get one tonight from a rancher up the road," Travis said. "He's got a couple of spares."

"Thanks. I appreciate it."

A knock at the door startled the little one and she ran to answer it. "I get it."

"Victoria." The warning note in Travis's voice had the girl pulling up short. "What did I tell you about answering the door?"

"Don't answer the door by mysef."

"That's correct."

Tori nodded. "Okay, Travis, you can come, too."

Sam smiled. Cute kid.

They returned from the front hallway a moment later with Violet from the diner, different without her apron and hair kerchief. Her hair fell in a straight, black satin wave down her back.

God, she was attractive.

She glanced around the room with her stunning violet eyes, settled on him briefly, then moved on.

"I brought you treats." To Tori, Rachel and Travis, she handed containers from her restaurant.

"Hey, parsnip soup," Travis said, enthusiastically. "Thanks, Vy."

Parsnip soup? Seriously? The guy was happy about parsnips?

Sam's distaste must have shown on his face because Travis laughed and said, "Don't knock it until you've tried it. It tastes better than it sounds."

Sam hoped so because it sounded awful.

He watched Violet and Rachel retreat to the kitchen, wishing he could find a reason to follow them. Sure, they were friends and probably just catching up on things, but what if one of them mentioned the fair?

When Violet actually mentioned his grandfather, his ears perked up.

"Carson said he wants to hear about our latest updates on the fair." Violet's voice faded as she entered the kitchen. "Told him…visit tomorrow…want to come?"

The rest was lost to him. He cast about for an excuse, anything, that would get him near the kitchen to eavesdrop. Of course, there wasn't a reason that would make sense.

How could he get close enough to the women to find out their intentions?

Before he came up with answers, Travis interrupted his thoughts.

"You mind joining me in the dining room?"

Sam followed him, where they sat at a long table. Travis started off with, "I don't mean to be rude, but you got any ID on you?"

Sam hesitated to show his New York driver's license

so instead he pulled his passport out of his shirt pocket. "I always carry this with me when I cross state lines."

Travis checked it out and nodded. He asked a series of questions designed to find out whether he could trust bringing a strange man into his home.

Sam respected that Travis wanted to protect his family. He would do anything to protect Chelsea, so he answered as best he could without giving too much away.

He explained that he'd recently gotten divorced and that—white lie—he hadn't felt comfortable continuing to work with his father-in-law.

Travis nodded as though that made perfect sense

He asked for a reference so Sam gave him John Raven's name and cell number. John knew his purpose here, so he would say all of the right things about Sam being a hard worker and trustworthy.

Sam also suspected Travis might not even make the call, and this was merely a formality to see whether Sam would produce references.

They returned to the living room where Travis watched Chelsea chat and play with Tori. Sam held his breath.

Finally, Travis said, "We need to get out to finish up today's chores."

Today? The guy wanted him to start work now?

"Sure," he said, wondering what *finishing up chores* meant.

"Bring your suitcase with you."

Apparently Chelsea made a good ambassador. Travis must think that a man who could raise a great kid like Chelsea wouldn't harm his children.

Sam retrieved his luggage from the front foyer. On his way to follow Travis, he passed the kitchen.

Violet came spinning out of the room with the baby in her arms, singing something silly. She ran smack-dab into

Sam. Instinctively, he dropped his suitcase and caught her before she fell.

A switch of electricity jolted him.

One of his arms snapped across her back while the other held one of her nicely rounded hips. Her curves a perfect temptation, she fit in his arms perfectly.

The sexy uptilt of black liner at the corners of her wide violet eyes made them look even larger and more striking. Sam was speechless for once in his life, and it seemed Violet was the same.

They stared, her coffee-scented breath fanning his face.

If he leaned close, he could place his mouth on the rapidly beating pulse throbbing in her neck.

He wanted to. Oh, yes.

Up close, her skin even more porcelain than he thought possible, the urge to kiss her flooded him.

Holy! She packed a punch.

A squirming bundle interrupted all of the warm sensations. He'd forgotten about the baby.

This woman rattled his brain.

Sam released Violet reluctantly.

Shaken, he joined Travis.

Travis pointed to a small bedroom at the back of the house across from what looked like a mudroom and laundry room.

"We have a bedroom upstairs for Chelsea," Travis said.

So Sam had been relegated to a spot far away from the rest of the family upstairs. It made perfect sense. In Travis's shoes, Sam would do the same thing.

"There's a washroom you can use on the far side of the kitchen. There's no bath, but there is a shower stall."

Sam nodded. "Good."

"We need to get to those chores," Travis said.

They stepped outside through a back door. Sam sensed

Violet following but she stopped in the screened-in porch and stayed there. Travis continued across a yard to a barn out back where a couple of horses munched on hay.

Sam felt Violet's gaze boring into his back.

"Half of the herd won't be delivered until tomorrow, but let's put the horses to bed for the night."

"What does that entail?" Sam could have bitten his own tongue. A cowboy would know that. "I mean, what are your systems here?"

Systems? Cowboys didn't talk about systems. Get your head out of business mode, Sam, and into ranching mode or you'll find yourself in deep shit.

Travis handed him a pitchfork. "Clear out their manure," Travis said, handing the tool to Sam. "We'll leave them with fresh bedding for the night."

Great. Shoveling manure. His worst nightmare. Back home, he had people to take care of his horse and Chelsea's pony. He knew what had to be done, but he'd never had to clean up after their horses in his whole life. What was he doing here in the back of beyond pretending to be something so far from his normal, sane self?

Gramps. Keep Gramps in mind and you'll get through this.

Drifting from the screened-in porch at the back of the house came a husky feminine laugh that could only belong to Violet. Probably laughing at his expense.

He glanced out of the open barn doors. Yep. She could see him. And his pitchfork. She knew exactly what his chore was.

"WHAT ARE YOU laughing at?" Rachel had come up beside Vy.

Vy averted her eyes away from Rachel. Her friend could read her too easily and she really didn't want Rachel to detect Vy's arousal after that encounter with Sam. Surely she would note her fast-beating pulse and her widened pupils. Weren't those signs of sexual attraction?

If Vy's pupils weren't dilated after having those long fingers on her body, she'd commit herself to a nunnery.

Sam delivered a feverish carnal impact simply by touching her hip and back.

For a moment, she'd thought he actually meant to kiss her and, in that unguarded instant, she would have welcomed it.

Stranger or not, and clearly a liar, Sam pulled her in. She'd wanted that kiss…and that angered her.

Self-defense kicking in gangbusters, she stood out here laughing at the man so she wouldn't march into the stable, haul him into a stall and have her way with him.

And wasn't that just the most ridiculous thing?

"Travis has Sam shoveling manure," she said, voice hard-edged so Rachel wouldn't realize how Sam's touch unnerved Vy.

"You're mean." Rachel softened the sentiment with a laugh. "Who knows? He might turn out to be all right with a little experience."

"What did you think of him?"

"He isn't being completely honest, of course. That man isn't a cowboy. Obviously." Rachel took the baby from Vy and settled her on her shoulder. "Here's the thing, though. I don't know what's going on, but I don't think he's evil or bad. Look at the way his daughter dealt with Tori. She could have just brushed her off, but she played with her. She's in the living room painting her toenails, for gosh sake. That man is a good father."

"I like the girl. I'm withholding judgment on the father. Why is he here?"

"That's the million-dollar question, isn't it?"

Travis approached the back porch with a frown marring his handsome brow.

He opened the door. "What's going on?" He directed the question toward Vy. "Why did you send me someone who's never held a pitchfork in his life?"

"I'm sorry," Rachel said. "I should have explained the whole story. Vy thinks that man's here for some nefarious purpose."

Travis swung his bright baby blues between Rachel and Vy. "So you sent him out to live in my house, with my family?"

It did look bad. "I don't think he's dangerous. God. I'd never do that to you and Rach."

"Then why is he here?" He turned to Rachel. "And why did you allow it?"

Vy answered. "Because he's a fraud and I want to see him get his just deserts."

"Why? Do you know him from somewhere else?"

She shook her head. "I've never met him before in my life."

"Then why are you so intent on making a fool out of him? You have any idea how hard that is on a person?"

Yes, she did. She'd made a fool of herself just a few minutes ago turning all moony and big eyed in Sam's embrace.

She bypassed the issue and said, "I don't sense any harm in him."

"Vy, neither do I, but I want to know what's going on."

"I can't explain. I would if I could. Can I just ask you to go along? Please?"

"I'll keep him on but I don't like laughing at people behind their backs. It doesn't sit well with me."

"Okay. I'll try to be more careful."

Travis left to return to the stable.

"He's right," Rachel said. "We shouldn't be so gleeful about embarrassing a stranger."

"I'll take on that role completely on my own. Travis can be mad at me instead of with you."

She straightened away from the porch post.

"I should get back to the diner."

They walked through the house where the two girls giggled while Chelsea painted Tori's fingernails. At her car, Vy threw her arms around Rachel and the baby. "Love you to bits, Rach. Thanks for doing this."

Vy stared at the poor trailer across the road, abandoned and forlorn in the cold March afternoon.

"I'm glad you got out of that thing." Her fervent whisper had her friend staring at her. Vy ignored Rachel's regard.

Rachel wouldn't let it go, though. "What happened, Vy? All of those years ago?"

"It doesn't matter. It's ancient history." She opened her car door but didn't get in. "Do you ever wonder why we're such good friends?"

"Because we love each other?"

"Yes, but *why*?"

Rachel looked a bit lost.

"Because of our histories," Vy said. "I mean, they aren't exactly the same, but parts of them are. We *get* each other, Rachel."

"True. We couldn't be closer if we were related."

"Like it is with Nadine and Honey and Max, too. We have these weird commonalities in our pasts. You're right about being related, as if we're drawn together like sisters."

Vy had given it a lot of thought. It was more than their pasts. They were all distinctly different, yet big parts of their personalities intersected.

They gave so much of themselves to others. Like with the fair. They busted their butts to bring it back to save the town. They'd made personal sacrifices. They gave from their hearts. Sometimes Vy wondered if they shared too much. If they kept giving away these chunks of themselves, what would be left of them in the end?

Beth fussed and Rachel patted her back. "You're in an odd mood today, Vy. What's bringing all of this up?"

"I don't know. I've just been thinking a lot lately." She stared across the road. Rachel followed her gaze.

"About trailers?"

"Among other things. I'm glad your life has changed. I guess I wish "

"You wish...?"

Vy shrugged off her blues. "Nothing. Everything's great."

She couldn't explain her mood to Rachel when she couldn't figure it out for herself.

"Gotta go." She jumped into her car and drove away. Better to bury herself in work than to try to come up with answers to questions she couldn't begin to articulate.

Chapter Four

Sam left his cowboy boots on the back porch.

He should have gone cheap, but no. As always, he'd wanted the best.

The best were now ruined, covered in manure and straw and who knew what else? Maybe they wouldn't be considered ruined to a cowboy. After all, the boots had been crafted to be used in this way, but Sam kept his boots and shoes polished.

In the first-floor washroom, he washed his face and hands, but his entire body itched.

He found Rachel in the kitchen with the baby in some kind of seat on the floor, alone, thank goodness. He wouldn't have to face the unsettling force of his attraction to Vy.

"I forgot to ask about arrangements. Should Chelsea and I head into town for dinner?"

"No need. You'll eat here with us. I'll just ask that you contribute to the grocery bills." She had a nice smile, warm and genuine. Not the least bit mean-spirited like a certain diner owner's. "If you like to eat anything exotic, I'm afraid you'll have to pick it up and cook it on your own. I can tell you where to shop."

"I'd appreciate it."

She chopped vegetables at the counter.

"Do you need help?"

"You look hot. Would you like to shower before dinner?"

"I'd like it above all things. Is there time?"

"You've got about half an hour. Travis is out front readying the barbecue for steaks. That man sure does love his steaks." Her laugh lifted a man's spirits. Lucky Travis.

"Where's Chelsea?"

"In her room with Tori."

"Do you mind if I go up to see her after I shower?"

Rachel looked surprised by his request, or rather that he'd requested it. "Of course you can visit Chelsea."

"Thanks." He showered and headed upstairs, noting how they creaked. Another smart move on Travis's part. No way could a man sneak upstairs in the middle of the night to harm his family without Travis hearing it. Sam respected that.

Chelsea lay on her stomach on her bed, with Tori on her stomach beside her. She was reading a children's book to the girl.

"Is everything okay?" He might appreciate what the rancher was doing for him but he didn't want them to think of Chelsea as an automatic babysitter.

"I'm good." She'd toned down the attitude, maybe because of the child.

"I'm good, too," the little one added, and Sam smiled. "Want to come listen? Chels reads real good."

"Yes, she does. I remember." She used to read all of her books out loud from the moment she learned how to read, until she grew old enough for chapter books and withdrew into them.

"Are you okay spending time with the little one?"

"Yes, I'm good."

"I'm good, too, Sam," Tori said again, a little mimic.

Sam winked at Chelsea and she responded with a smile, shared amusement at Tori's cuteness. Nice.

He went downstairs to his minuscule bedroom to unpack his clothes into the small dresser and closet.

Minutes later, conversation and laughter flowed from the kitchen. Aromas whispered down the hallway. Steak and potatoes. The sounds and scents of homey contentment... A state foreign to him.

Sam entered the kitchen, where he found the family scene calming. Chelsea sat at the table blowing bubbles for the baby. Travis leaned against the refrigerator. Tori hung upside down from Travis's strong hands, her heels against his chest, her back to his knees and her blond curls hanging and nearly touching the floor.

"Look what I can do, Sam."

"That's quite a trick."

She tossed her legs toward the floor and Travis flipped her upright, steadying her with a hand on her head.

Rachel put the finishing touches on a salad and handed it to her husband.

"Okay, let's eat. Everyone to the dining room."

He sat on one side of the table while Travis and Rachel took the ends. Tori insisted that Chelsea sit beside her.

Chelsea seemed fine with the arrangement, but it left Sam feeling oddly alone.

Something stirred inside of him. A wish. A longing. A...*something*. He didn't recognize what he felt or what he wanted, and that frustrated him.

He thought he was a man who knew his own mind, but his world had been turned upside down. He lived in a state of flux. Maybe he'd jumped on this opportunity to help his grandfather so he could avoid his uncertainty about the future. He could make his new venture work once it went live next month, but business offered no guarantees, no matter how smart you were. No one could control the market.

But life was about risk.

And these days, for Sam, it was also about revenge. That revenge would take the form of making millions and, however he could, bringing down Tiff's company.

He caught Chelsea watching him with a frown. Could she read his mind? Did she know he wanted to see his ex-wife and former father-in-law fail? After all, it had been Sam's initiatives that had made their joint company a success.

More power to them if they thought Colin Dewers, Tiffany's new husband, could bring in the money Sam had. Sam wasn't arrogant, just realistic.

Getting his mind off the frustration of waiting for a launch that was still a month off, he gazed around the room he hadn't really noticed during his "interview" earlier.

Normal furniture, a dark table with fake leather parson's chairs, echoed the style throughout the rest of the house. The furniture in the entire place combined probably cost less than what Tiffany had spent on just their living room. And yet these people achieved what Tiffany had completely missed. Comfort. Coziness.

Once the food had been passed around and plates were full, Sam realized the comfort and coziness came from far more than the furniture and the house. It originated with Rachel and Travis. They exuded happiness.

Their down-home welcoming charm contrasted with the high-toned atmosphere of both his former and his current home in New York by miles. Maybe he shouldn't have hired a decorator. Maybe he should have done it himself.

Chelsea had managed to make her room her own, with posters and glow-in-the-dark galaxies on her ceiling and stuff piled around her room.

Perhaps he needed to relax his neat-freak tendencies to have a place for everything and everything in its place. It might provide him with a modicum of calm, but it also left his homes bereft of charm.

Rachel laughed at something Travis said, bringing Sam back to his mission. The town fair and rodeo.

Braced to broach the subject, Sam opened his mouth but Rachel spoke first.

"We got another ride set up and ready to go, the old teacup ride for the children. You should see the paint job. It's beautiful and whimsical." She wiped a dribble of milk from Tori's chin. "Unfortunately, the Zipper was beyond repair. A shame, really. It's a classic ride."

"Yeah," Travis said. "I heard. I'll head over on the weekend to check progress on the rides."

Sam's curiosity would make perfect sense in this conversation.

"Teacup ride? Zipper?" he asked, leaving the question open so Rachel would answer however she pleased.

"If you drive just west of town, you'll notice the Rodeo Fairgrounds."

"Chelsea and I did a tour of the local roads before we came to your place. We saw it. A great place, but it looked odd, a mix of old and new. There were people working there. What was all of the activity about? You planning to have a fair sometime soon?"

Chelsea kicked him under the table. No doubt about it, he was going to hell for lying in front of his daughter.

What choice did he have? He'd had to bring Chelsea with him to Rodeo.

Not true, Sam. Not completely.

In all honesty, he'd wanted time with Chelsea to see whether they could get back to the fun, loving relationship they'd had before Tiffany had thrown a curveball at both of them.

Nowadays, the woman wanted time to spend with her new husband. Sam recognized Chelsea's unhappiness with her mother. Chelsea didn't like hanging out at Tiffany's house so she lived with Sam. He liked it that way and wanted it to be permanent. He had lawyers working on that now.

Infidelity affected more than just the spouse. Chelsea had felt betrayed, too.

She had been acting out ever since, Her strict private school had offered an ultimatum: get her help or get her out of the school. For a child who'd performed well until this year, it was devastating.

The only consolation was that the timing had been right to take her on this road trip to see her grandfather. Sam had thought, hoped, *prayed* that they could connect again and return to the goofy fun they used to have, but all the long miles had done was separate them further.

Now this business of helping out Gramps had pushed them to new extremes of separation.

His frustration made his steak taste like sawdust. Sam couldn't wait to get this over with, to return home and hire her a tutor for the summer. That, along with the assignments she handed in online, might save her year.

Chelsea watched him with mutiny threatening on her brow.

Please, his expression implored. *Be quiet. Let me do this my way.*

He'd give anything to bring her life back to normal, but normal was a flexible commodity these days.

"The town is reviving our old amusement park," Rachel said. "It ran every summer, passed from one generation to the next, for nearly a hundred years before the current owner had to give it up."

"Why did he give it up? Financial concerns?"

"I don't think so. That was fifteen years ago. Carson was getting on. He's almost ninety now. It's a lot of work for one man. No one else seemed inclined to take on the job at the time."

"So why didn't he just sell it?"

"It has a lot of sentimental value for him. I'm not sure, but I think he always hoped his grandson from back east would come out and revive it. No chance of that, though."

Odd tone in her voice. Displeasure. Implied criticism. They didn't even know him and they disapproved. Did Sam want to question it and find out what the townspeople thought of him?

"Why no chance?" Chelsea asked, watching him to gauge his expression. *Thanks, kid.*

"It seems that Carson and his grandson are two completely different characters. The grandson would never deign to grace our small town. I think he's a snob."

"Careful," Travis cautioned. "You've never met the man. For all we know, he could be just fine."

Rachel relented. "I know. I'm kind of promoting clichés, aren't I?"

"Sure are. Plenty of city people are fine."

"I know, Travis. I just get so pi—" She glanced at Tori quietly using a fork to mash a puddle of butter into her hot potatoes. "I get angry. He broke Carson's heart."

Broke his heart!

"When I think that he could have come out here any time in the past fifteen years to help out his grandfather— ooh, I get so mad."

Stunned, Sam sat back. He would have come out if he'd known it was more than just Gramps wanting to retire. He hadn't known he was breaking his heart by not visiting. Why hadn't Gramps told him he had expectations of Sam? But what expectations? That he would give up his life in Manhattan and his career?

He'd never promised Gramps that. He'd never even hinted at it.

Chelsea watched him with the worried frown she wore too often these days. He wished he understood what went on in her newly formed teenage brain.

"Forget the grandson," Travis said. "Why didn't Carson's son ever visit?"

"That was before my time," Rachel replied. "I don't know the whole story but there was a scandal before he left town."

What? What?

"What was it?" Travis asked.

Thank you!

"I know only the gossip and not much of it but it has to do with Candace Bolton."

Who is she? Sam wanted to ask.

"Who is she?" Travis asked.

Good man.

"She's a widow who lives on the other side of town. Nice lady, but keeps to herself. That's all I know, Travis. Something happened between Carson II and Candace. He left town to study out east. He never came home again."

"Too bad for Carson."

"The first, you mean? *Our* Carson? Yeah. I think he missed his son a lot. Oh, well, water under the bridge."

Getting off the topic of how horrible his father had been in not coming home and how terrible a grandson Sam had been by not visiting, Sam asked, "Why are you bringing the fair back now if it's been closed for so many years?"

"My friends and I decided it was time. As in most small

towns without industry to support the citizens, our young people are leaving to find jobs elsewhere." She offered him more salad. He shook his head. "The park, all of that land and the amazing machines on it are going to ruin. We're bringing it back to life and hoping to employ a lot of locals."

Yeah, the land and the machines, all leased for only a dollar.

"It's been tough, though," Travis cut in. "Because there isn't a lot of money in town to make it happen. Rachel and her friends are donating all of their labor. They won't make a cent."

Sam didn't believe that for one minute. Once the fair and rodeo turned a profit this summer, they'd rake in all kinds of cash. And Gramps had no memory of what percentage of that profit he was entitled to receive. What a mess.

"Tomorrow's Saturday," Rachel said, changing the subject.

Darn. He couldn't bring it back around without seeming suspicious.

"It's our family tradition to go to the diner for breakfast," Rachel said. "Would you like to join us?"

"Say yes, Dad."

Sam looked at his daughter. Sad to say, he no longer trusted her. She seemed to have an ulterior purpose for everything she wanted these days. But then, he'd skulked around issuing untruths to people who seemed to be honest.

But he couldn't trust anyone in this town, could he? Not until he knew them better.

Even so, how could a trip to town cause problems? Unable to think of a reason to say no, he nodded.

Travis cut in. "You and I'll go out to the stable at dawn to take care of the animals."

Travis skewered another steak for himself.

"After breakfast, you can take the morning off, but be back here by two. I'm expecting half of my new herd. I'll need help getting them off the trucks and out into the field."

"Sure thing."

"I called my friend. He has only one horse to spare at the moment. He's a bit rowdy, but you should be good with him for herding tomorrow."

Okay. He could do that. He knew how to ride. He and his friends were part of an amateur polo league. He'd watched videos of cowboys directing cows. *Cattle, Sam. They call them cattle out here, not cows.*

First, a good night's sleep. This deception business exhausted him.

IT TOOK A while to get the Read family going, especially since one of them was an infant who needed everything from wipes to diapers to…whatever else was in that big bag Rachel carried.

The diner was hopping. It seemed that everyone and his uncle came out for Saturday breakfast. Maybe hardworking ranchers and cowboys set aside this time to socialize.

He suspected cowboys did their raucous socializing on Friday and Saturday nights at the bar at the end of the strip, Honey's Place, but kept it civilized at the diner. Family time.

The Read family and Sam and Chelsea waited twenty minutes for a window booth for six to clear out.

Violet hustled like a whirling dervish with coffeepots and menus. She never lost her cool, though, she even joked and laughed with her customers despite the need for speed.

Sam watched her, fascinated and wary. The woman might have a curvy body, but sharp edges defined her personality. With him, at any rate.

She came to take their orders, giving him no more attention than anyone else at the table. In fact, he received less than the others, surprising after last night's bump in the kitchen.

Maybe she hadn't been as affected as him.

Or maybe she had. He'd thought so. Maybe she'd faked being immune to him this morning.

She didn't even look at him. It bothered him. But why should it? She meant nothing to him.

"What'll you folks have?"

After the Reads ordered, Chelsea asked if she could have a Western omelet without onions.

"Sure thing. Do you want green or red peppers?"

"Aren't green peppers traditional in a Western?" Chelsea asked.

"So are onions," Violet retorted. "Besides, we aren't too traditional in this diner. Haven't you noticed? We're classic, but with a twist."

"Red, then." Chelsea smiled, a white slash surrounded by purple lipstick.

"Nice lipstick," Violet said.

Sam shot her a look meant to imply, "Don't encourage her."

Chelsea caught it and scowled. Violet laughed.

Two against one again. Unfair.

"Last, but not least, Mr. Michaels, what can I get for you?"

He almost missed that *he* was Mr. Michaels. "I'll have the Good and Hearty Cowboy Breakfast, Violet." He refused to use the shortened *Vy.* Too small for a woman with a big personality; he didn't like it. Besides, he liked *Violet* a lot. It was old-fashioned, even if the woman wasn't, and pretty, like the woman *definitely* was.

Today she wore a green dress with small black polka dots, fitted over her bodice and embracing a fine set of hips. A white kerchief wrapped around her head reminded him of iconic images of Rosie the Riveter. A black apron completed the look.

"The Cowboy Breakfast is a good start to the day for the manliest of cowboys," she responded and walked away, taking the menus with her.

Rachel looked anywhere but at him.

Travis cocked his head and frowned.

Sam wanted to throttle the woman.

Chelsea giggled, then looked worried. "You aren't going to flirt with Vy today, are you, Dad?"

"What if I was?"

"Just don't be cheesy about it, okay?"

"Cheesy? And here I wanted to compliment her on being full-bodied like a fine Italian wine."

Rachel laughed, but Chelsea gasped. "That is *so* corny, Dad."

She didn't realize he was kidding. "It suits her."

"She's coming back." Chelsea's eyes flicked past him. "Don't do it."

"Hmm" was all he said. His daughter had been laughing at his expense too much lately. Time for a little payback.

Violet poured coffee all around.

Sam watched his daughter doctor hers with too much sugar and cream. Just as she took a sip, he said, "Sure wish it was late enough in the day for a glass of wine. A *full-bodied* wine."

Chelsea choked on her coffee. Sam patted her back.

"Something go down the wrong way, honey? Maybe you're not ready for coffee. It's really a grown-up beverage."

Rachel laughed softly.

Violet cast Sam a puzzled look before tending to the next table.

Chelsea covered her face with her napkin and coughed. When she got her breath back, she said, "I'm going to get you for that, Dad."

"You and whose army?"

She rolled her eyes. "Old-fashioned, Dad. So outdated." She sounded tough but the smallest of smiles hovered at the edges of her mouth.

Nice. Sam liked teasing her.

After breakfast, they went their separate ways in their own vehicles, the Reads in their old pickup and he and Chelsea in his SUV.

They headed first to the mall on the highway. If Sam was going to work full-time for Travis doing dirty jobs, he needed to own more than one pair of jeans.

If yesterday were any indication, he'd be doing laundry daily. He should set up a payment plan for using electricity and water while living with the Reads.

He liked them.

In a clothing store, he picked up four more pairs of jeans, one for every day of the week. On the weekends, he could wear his chinos, as he'd done today.

"Should I get another pair of cowboy boots?" he asked Chelsea.

She shrugged. "You're the fake cowboy. Not me."

"Ha. Ha. Keep your voice down," he whispered. "I might not be a real one, but I'm dead serious about saving Granmps from those women."

She frowned. "I don't know, Dad. The two women we've met so far are really nice."

Nice wasn't the first word that came to mind when he

thought of Violet. "Yes, they seem okay, but Gramps is worried, so…here we are."

"Gramps is old. Do you think maybe his mind could be going? Maybe his judgment is wrong."

Sam frowned. "He was definitely different yesterday. I'm worried they might have taken advantage of his new-found bewilderment. I'm worried about his mind. He used to be a sharp businessman. It's hard to understand how he could just agree to this without signing a contract and that he can't remember how much of the profits he'll be entitled to."

He picked up a half-dozen denim shirts to take to the lone clerk at the cash register. "Those women will make a lot of tourist dollars from the rodeo and fair. That money should belong to the Carmichaels."

Sam kept his voice low so no one would hear him. Probably unnecessary. The store was close to empty.

"What if they're telling the truth, though, and it's all going back into the town?"

"Shouldn't Gramps still get a percentage?"

"Rachel and Vy seem honest to me, Dad."

"Rachel, definitely. Violet, no. She's got something up her sleeve. Trust me. I've met her type in business. She's hiding something."

"How do you know?"

"Intuition."

After Sam paid for his purchases, they left the shop and passed the boot store.

"So? Should I get more boots?"

"Let's go see Gramps again," Chelsea said.

"I'm taking that as a no to another pair of boots."

"Did you notice the boots Travis was wearing this morning?" she asked.

"No. What were they?"

"They looked a bit old, but all polished up. I think they're, like, his good boots that he saves for, like, church and stuff. He also has an incredibly ancient pair beside the back door."

"So I should get a pair for wearing into town?"

"Yeah, if you want to fit in. I mean, today you're looking preppy, Dad. Blue button-down, beige slacks, conservative shoes. How many cowboys did you see in the restaurant dressed like that?"

None. Damn. "Okay, let's go find me a pair of nice boots. I ruined my expensive ones yesterday and this morning."

"And another thing, Dad. Do *not* iron your jeans like you did before you came here. Talk about being old-fashioned."

Sam studied her with a frown. "I didn't. I've never touched an iron in my life. Why do you think I did?"

"*Hello?* The sharp creases in them?"

"That wasn't me. That was the dry cleaner."

She stared. "You sent your jeans to the dry cleaner?"

"Susan did, along with a couple of my suits."

"She's a good housekeeper and usually on the ball. So why didn't she just throw them in the washer and dryer?"

"I told her they were stiff because they were new. She said she'd take care of them. That's all I know."

They stepped into a Western shoe store.

"Ooh, look at these, Dad. Snakeskin."

"Maybe if I sang in a rock band," he scoffed. "Here. These look good. Dark blue with gray leather insets."

"I like those."

After purchasing them, on their way out of the mall, Chelsea stopped in front of a nail salon. "Wait. I want to go in here."

"You want to get your nails done? I need to help unload Travis's herd at two. If we want to visit Gramps first—"

"I won't be long. I want to buy nail polish for Tori. I think she'd like sparkles, don't you?"

Like a slow-moving sunrise, a smile spread across Sam's face. "You used to."

Chelsea echoed his smile. "Remember how much Mom hated it?"

"She thought it was crass."

"Yeah, she did, but you fought to let me have it."

"Girls just want to have fun, Chelsea."

"Remember how much I used to like that song?"

"You played it over and over and over again."

She giggled and it sounded heavenly.

"Look! Hot-pink with silver sparkles. Tori will *love* this. I'll need some more nail polish remover, too."

Sam slipped her a twenty out of his pocket.

By the time they left the mall and got onto the road to drive to the old-folks' home, a mild drizzle had started.

Sam turned into the driveway and immediately pulled a U-turn back out of the parking lot.

"Why are you turning around?" Chelsea asked. "I want to see Gramps."

"Didn't you see who was there?"

"Where?"

"Heading into the building. Violet and Rachel with some other women. What do you want to bet that's the organizing committee? They might be going in to see your grandfather."

"So what, Dad?"

He stopped on the shoulder down the road.

"So…" he answered Chelsea with exaggerated patience. "We can't go in while they're here or they'll figure out who I am."

Chelsea slumped in her seat and crossed her arms, becoming belligerent again, the camaraderie of this morning's happy shopping trip gone.

"Why would that be bad?" she asked. "We could go in there right now and get everything cleared up. You could ask all your questions and they could answer them."

"That's not how things are done. In business, you hold your position until you have all of the facts. I don't have those yet. I don't have *anything*." He banged his hand on the steering wheel. "You don't let opponents know what you're doing until it's already done."

"This isn't business."

"It sure is, sweetheart. Trust me. I know."

"I don't think you do," she mumbled while Sam wished he were a fly on the wall inside his grandfather's room.

What were those women telling him?

Chapter Five

Vy entered Carson Carmichael's room with Rachel, Nadine and Max, and the newest addition to their team, Samantha Read.

He greeted them with his trademark crooked grin. "Ladies! Good to see you. It warms an old man's heart to see such bright flowers on a gray day."

Seeing Carson a pure pleasure for Vy, she loved his quirky sense of humor, his intelligence and even his corny flirtation.

She handed him the cup of rice pudding with raisins that she'd brought for him, along with a spoon.

"Rice pudding! My favorite."

She'd brought it knowing that. Lately, he'd been saying the same thing every time she visited. She frowned. He never used to repeat himself.

"Vy, you're a doll." He dug in right away.

She warned, "We have to get down to business right away. I have only an hour. Breakfast rush is over, but I can't leave for too long on a Saturday. Will would kill me if I missed lunch service."

"You're the boss, not Will. He's only your cook." A spot of cream dribbled down Carson's chin. Food stains dotted his sweater. Vy remembered a time when Carson dressed in gray snakeskin cowboy boots, a white Stetson and a pink string tie, the nattiest cowboy around. "Can't you set your own hours?"

Vy wouldn't wound his pride by wiping his chin, but she wanted to. In his better days, he would have hated to look like this. "Yep," she responded, "But I'm a *responsible* boss. I don't skip out on my cook on my busiest day. Let's get down to business. Who wants to start?"

As coordinator of the amusement rides and the person responsible for bringing them up to code, Rachel spoke up first.

"We have sixty percent of the rides up and running. I already showed you photos of the carousel, Carson. You should see the teacup ride. It's like something out of *Alice in Wonderland*." She whipped out her cell phone. "Look. I took a couple of shots for you. Swipe like this to see them all."

Carson took the phone in his veined hand and followed her instructions. His eyes turned moist.

"So damned beautiful. Pardon my language. Who painted it so nicely?"

"Zach Brandt."

"Man's got a lot of talent."

"He sure does. Like all of us, he donated his services."

At the mention of Zach, Nadine turned away to stare out the window.

A good guy who came into the diner regularly, Zach had sold Vy the paintings that hung on her walls. Why would the mention of his name spark tension in Nadine? At times like this, Vy regretted that she hadn't grown up in town. She missed chunks of her friends' backgrounds.

Of all five women, Nadine was the second-most private person of the group. First was Maxine, who was tight and often withdrawn.

On second thought, knowing the secrets Vy had kept

from the girls, one in particular was a doozy, she couldn't fault anyone else for not being forthcoming.

Rachel caught her phone just as it slipped from Carson's fingers.

"We had to dismantle the Zipper." Rachel tucked the phone into her purse. "It was just too far gone."

"Zipper," he murmured, but Vy got the impression he wasn't sure what Rachel was talking about.

She and Rachel exchanged glances. They'd been worried about Carson and his faulty memory.

Vy moved the proceedings along. "Nadine, do you want to give a report?"

As secretary of the board, Nadine Campbell also handled advertising and promotion. She turned out as always with impeccable makeup, a curtain of long straightened red hair fell down her back.

It was naturally curly but Nadine disliked her curls.

"I'll post ads in all of the papers in the major cities of the neighboring states," Nadine said. "North and South Dakota, Nebraska, Wyoming, Colorado, Idaho, Washington and Oregon. I'd like to reach as many small towns as possible, too. It's pricey, though. We'll see how far the money goes."

"I could—"

Nadine cut Carson off. "I don't mean to be rude, but we can't take your money. Keep your savings for yourself."

Vy added, "You've done so much for us already by leasing the land to us so cheaply. We couldn't do any of this without your cooperation. Your initial investment was crucial and started the ball rolling on fixing the rides. Taking only a small portion of the profits is risky. It doesn't seem fair. What if we don't make a profit? You'll have made nothing and will have lost your initial investment."

Again, Carson looked momentarily confused but then

shrugged. "Then I'll have made nothing. This event isn't about me. It's about bringing money into the town and creating jobs."

He took a sip of water from a glass at his elbow. "The park and land were sitting there doing nothing for me, anyway. I got a lifetime of pleasure out of running it. Out of making people happy every summer."

"You made me happy," Rachel said. "Every year, it was one of my favorite childhood times."

One of her few good ones, Vy thought, but didn't voice aloud. Rachel's memories were hers to share at her own discretion.

"I don't mind the next generation taking over," Carson said. "It pleases me to have y'all bring the park back to life."

As one, they nodded.

Carson eased up on one hip and pulled his wallet out of his pocket. He counted his bills. It looked like about a hundred dollars.

Vy glanced around at all uneasily. What was he doing?

He took out a couple of ten-dollar bills and tried to hand them to Nadine.

"Carson," she said. "I can't take your money."

"Buy more ads. Get more people."

Oh, Carson, thought Vy, *what's happening to you?* He had no idea how little twenty dollars was worth where advertising was concerned. But he must have known at one time. He used to advertise.

She curled her fingers around Carson's. "Thank you, but put your money away. You've given us so much already. We'll take over from here."

Carson tucked the money back into his billfold, but then took it all back out, counted his bills twice and then put it back away. Only then did he slide the wallet back into his pocket.

With a worried frown, Vy turned to Max. "How about you? How are your plans coming along?"

Maxine Porter, self-conscious and quiet, shifted where she leaned against the doorway.

"Carson, you ran the rodeo for years and I appreciated how much fun it was," Max started, "but I want to do something different with this new incarnation of the fair." As determinedly unfeminine as Max was, her voice always came as a shock, both husky and smoky.

She shoved her hands into her front pockets and hunched her shoulders up around her ears. Max hated being the center of attention.

Carson turned to her with interest. "Different how?"

"I want to temper how hard the traditional rodeo is on the animals. First off, I want to cut out bull riding."

Carson's brows nearly hit his receding hairline. "Bull riding's popular. You'll disappoint both the riders and the audience."

"Not if I offer something different that's entertaining."

"But what, Maxine?"

She shuffled her feet, which meant only one thing to Vy. Max might be quiet, but she had strong opinions and a stronger backbone. Without meeting anyone's eyes, another sign she had funny business in mind, she said, "Um… I'm thinking really strange entertainment, like camel racing."

What? "Max, we need this rodeo to be a success," Vy said faintly. She'd thought they'd dissuaded her from doing anything rash.

Honey, Rachel and Nadine groaned. Samantha, still new to the group, maintained a neutral expression—almost. The slightest frown marred a Marilyn Monroe–perfect face.

"Camel…?" Carson leaned forward, jaw jutting. "Are

you loco? That ain't no Wild West animal. You'll have a revolt on your hands from all the cowboys expecting to take part in a real rodeo. Why would you go so strange?"

Max hunched her shoulders, defensive at the drop of a hat, as always. "*You* did."

"What do you mean? I ran a traditional rodeo."

Max gestured toward the phone Rachel still held in her hand. "Look at the animals in the photos of the carousel. Your ancestor didn't just stick to ponies. He used elk and bulls and bighorn sheep. White-tailed deer! Who puts elk and deer on a carousel ride? The park has a tradition of bucking tradition."

Carson covered his face with one palm. "This might be too far from the norm."

Max nodded. "I know, but I want a chance to try. Consider the entertainment value for families."

"Yep. It would be funny. Who're you going to get to ride them, though? You know most cowboys have more pride than to wrangle a camel, for God's sake."

"I know, but…" Max sighed. She'd had this argument already with all of them. They hadn't supported her. Now Carson withheld support, too.

"You can't do this, Max." Vy's voice as strained as her patience, she continued, "We *have* to make money this year. If we don't succeed, there won't be any more to follow. The town needs money. Our youth need jobs."

Max lifted her belligerent little chin. "I *know* that, Vy." She glared at all of them. "This will work. Why won't you trust me?"

"Because it's too different," Honey said quietly, the peacemaker trying to bring them back onto an even keel with her reasonable tone.

But Vy knew there was no reasoning with Maxine.

"Let's move on," Vy said, voice tight. They couldn't

have this fight in Carson's room. With one hard-edged look at Max, she let her know the issue wasn't settled, not by a long shot. "Samantha, how do the finances look?"

Vy hated to ask. They were chronically short of money.

"Not good. We have to do a lot more fund-raising. Much of the work of restoring the amusement park is being done by volunteers, but not all."

Samantha opened her laptop. "Any work that needs to be inspected by the state has to be done by professionals, i.e. electrical, mechanical, plumbing, and we have to pay for that. It's pricey. As Nadine mentioned, advertising is expensive."

"Food will be, too," Vy added. "I'll have to order mountains of food. I don't know how we'll come up with the cash we'll need."

"Presales of tickets," Samantha said. "They're slow right now. We're selling to locals only. With the strength of the park's past reputation, we can sell more, but it depends on how far people are willing to travel for rides and food." She glanced at Max. "And the rodeo."

Max stomped out of the room.

"Maxine!" Vy called. "Don't be like that. Come back."

She didn't.

"Sorry." Samantha closed her laptop.

Uptight and overwhelmed, Vy said, "Not your fault. Once Max gets ideas, she plows through. She doesn't have a clue how to change a course once she's started on it."

Thank goodness they stood in the relative privacy of Carson's room. It would have been awful if other townspeople had witnessed it. They needed to present a united front so people would have faith in the fair and rodeo.

"Let's talk about food," Samantha said, "so I'll have a better idea of costs there. What ideas have you come up with, Vy?"

Vy forced her thoughts away from Max and the possibility that she might screw up this entire operation. Her stomach cramped. "I thought we could do a fifties' theme, since that's what I'm used to cooking in the diner. People respond well to nostalgia. If you don't mind, Carson, I'd like to pick your brain about the kinds of things you used to sell back then."

"Corn dogs, hot dogs, burgers, candy floss. The usual amusement-park fare," Carson answered.

Vy nodded. "That's what I thought. I'll serve that kind of thing for nostalgic value but will update all of those, make them more sophisticated. People want higher-end food."

"Even rural communities?" Samantha asked.

"You've eaten in the diner. You've seen how I've updated everything. The townspeople love it. Not one person has ever come up to me and said, 'Make your mac and cheese bland like it used to be. Stop using that sharp white cheddar you order from Canada.' They like the bacon and jalapeños I add, too."

"But is it just that everyone local is used to your food?" Honey asked.

"I don't think so. Look at the proliferation of TV shows about cooking. Everybody watches Food Network. The other day, Lester Voile asked me to try a recipe idea he saw on *Chopped*. Said he didn't want to cook it at home but would eat it in the diner. Lester! Watching Food Network!"

"How will you handle the food during the fair?" Carson snapped to his old role of boss as though he'd never left. "Who'll do the cooking? Who'll serve?"

"I've given it a lot of thought. Fortunately, the fair will be only a week long, but that week will cover two weekends, when we will be the busiest."

Carson nodded.

"I've already put out the word that I'll need employees for that week as well as the week before. As expected, I've received a lot of job requests from teenagers. It's good for them. Many will make money to take away to college with them."

"That's good."

"It is, Carson, but the downside is that they have no experience with cooking, especially not for crowds. People are emotional about food. It needs to be cooked properly and served hot or cold as the case may be."

"Yep. Good points. So?"

"So I've approached several of the older women in town to manage all of these young people. They are excellent cooks and have already raised teenagers so they'll know how to deal with them."

"Sounds like a fine idea. I had half a dozen concession booths when I ran the fair. Large ones. Found I needed every one of them. You will, too, especially if you get a good turnout."

"We're being optimistic and assuming we'll have excellent attendance."

"You can judge your food needs by ticket sales," Honey interrupted, "but there could be nearly as many people who just show up without a prepurchased ticket. It's a tough call, Vy. How much food should you have on hand? How much will get sold? How much will go to waste?"

Vy rubbed her forehead. She'd never taken on such a big project in her life. "None of it will go to waste. Whatever doesn't get eaten will go to the townspeople."

"If it's given to them," Nadine interjected, "that will be a cost we'll have to bear."

"I know," Vy snapped, then reeled in her temper. Nadine only articulated what Vy already knew. "I'm sorry, Nadine. I shouldn't have been rude, but I worry."

"I know you do, Vy, which is why we're having this discussion. To figure out how to deal with potential problems. I have it easy with promotion. I'll spend only what I'm given. You, on the other hand, have to spend money on food that might not get sold. How can we make sure you don't lose money on the fair?"

"Good question," Carson said. "It wasn't so bad for me. I'd done it for years and ordered food each year according to what I'd sold the year before. But this is brand-new. It's been too many years since I held the fair. Will there be interest? Won't there?"

It was good to hear Carson back to his old sharp self. The thought had only just entered Vy's mind when he took his wallet out of his pocket again, counted his bills and then slipped it back away.

What on earth?

"We can't predict success," Rachel said quietly, ignoring Carson's actions. "We can only make our best guesses and hope we get it right."

"Last, but not least," Vy said, "Samantha has agreed to set up an operating budget for us. Another tough job."

"I can only do that," Samantha said, "if you can all give me projections of how much you'll need. I can tell you what we have right now from the two fund-raising dances." She named a figure that was impressive.

"The townspeople were generous," Nadine said. "Some bought ten or twelve tickets to the dances even when they were using only one or two. Honey provided all of the beer and liquor at cost, so all sales were pure profit. Thank you, Honey."

"It was my pleasure. You know I'm happy to make whatever contribution I can. Here's the thing, though. While that sounds like a lot of money, it's still depressingly low for putting on an event of this size."

Nods all around confirmed that everyone had been thinking the same thing.

"We can't hold any more dances," Honey said. "We'll be in danger of bleeding our town's residents dry, the very people we're restarting the fair to help."

"We have to be creative."

"How, Nadine?" Vy asked. "If we can't get more money from the town, where do we get it from?"

Nadine shook her head, bristling from Vy's hard tone. "I wish I had an answer for you."

Had they taken on more than they could do? God, Vy just didn't know. They were smart women used to hard work, but this job was huge.

Honey glanced at her watch. "You'd better get back to work, Vy."

Vy sighed. "Yeah. As always, Carson, you have my deepest gratitude for letting us use your land and rides for our event."

Carson's grin split his face into a network of wrinkles. "Pure pleasure for me, my dears. Thank you for visiting an old man and brightening his day with your lovely presence. You're darlings, every one of you."

Vy packed her container and spoon and kissed Carson's cheek. The others kissed him, too, and they all left.

They trudged out to their vehicles, saying goodbye with no small amount of frustration.

Max had already driven away in her old pickup.

Vy sighed. At some point she would have to get Max back in line with the rest of them. If only she had a clue how to do that.

As she drove away, she thought about how things had developed. They were all gung ho to put on a great fair and to hire local friends and families.

Let's put our friends and families to work to bring in much-needed salaries.

Rah, rah.

Let's attract tourists to fill the town's coffers.

Rah, rah.

Let's put Rodeo, Montana, back on the map.

Rah, rah, rah.

Then reality had set in, along with nerves and panic.

Could they bring this off? Or would they all be bank-rupt by the end of August?

She drove down the highway back to Rodeo. An empty vehicle parked on the side of the road caught her eye. It looked like that big SUV Sam Michaels drove.

Couldn't be. What would he be doing way out here? Spying on her? Not likely. The man would have no reason to. He didn't know her from Adam.

Must be someone from up the road cutting through the bush to get to Sandy River to fish.

Sam's handsome image arose in her mind, but she squashed it ruthlessly.

"Daaad, I can't breathe. Let me up."

Sam's hand on the back of his daughter's head held it down to her knees. His own head was out of sight on the gearshift. Awkward and uncomfortable, but necessary.

"Be quiet. Hold on a minute. I want to make sure they're gone."

He waited another few minutes to be certain and then peeked up through the windshield.

"All gone." He released Chelsea so she could sit up.

"That was juvenile," the juvenile said, "hiding in our car like we're criminals."

"Until I know what's going on with these women, this is the way it has to be." His tone brooked no opposition, but Chelsea, being Chelsea and a new teenager, disagreed with him, anyway.

"I hate it. I hate telling lies and being dishonest, Dad."

He softened. "Believe it or not, so do I, but I'm going to protect Gramps in any way I can. Let's go see him and find out whether those women are up to mischief."

Minutes later, Sam entered his grandfather's room dreading what he would find. If those women had upset him there would be hell to pay.

Instead, Gramps sat staring out the window with a smile on his face. Happy. Content.

"How did the meeting go?" Sam asked his grandfather.

"What meeting?" he countered, seeming to wonder seriously what Sam was talking about.

Sam stopped in his tracks. "With the bevy of beauties who left here five minutes ago."

The older man looked as though he was searching empty memory banks. Then he brightened. "Oh, that meeting." Gramps smiled. "They are beautiful girls, aren't they?"

"Gramps…"

"Yes?"

Sam swallowed his frustration. "What did they want?"

By the frown on Gramps's face, he had to search fraying memory banks again. "They wanted to talk about the fair. Some funny ideas, though."

Unease skittered through Sam. "What ideas?"

Gramps thought for a moment before he spoke. "Um… Vy and Honey are smart businesswomen. They'll make solid decisions where food and beverages go."

Sam kept his opinion to himself about Violet.

"Nadine's going to advertise. If she had a bigger budget, she'd get more ticket sales. I offered more money, but—"

"What?" Sam cut him off. "You offered *money*? It's your property. It's your equipment. *They* should be paying

you." Was Gramps going senile? Sam should have come here a couple of years ago to check up on him. Then he wouldn't have fallen prey to those schemers. Sam cursed the upheaval in his own life that had everything falling apart. He'd not been free until now.

His grandfather took out his wallet and counted his money. "One hundred dollars. I wanted to give them twenty. Nadine wouldn't take it."

Twenty dollars? Sam had thought he'd meant he'd offered some of his life savings. Did Gramps really think that twenty dollars would make a dent in any advertising Nadine had planned?

Nadine hadn't accepted it. A sign of honesty? Or disdain for so little?

Gramps counted the money again, then put it away. He stared at Sam.

"I'm safe now that you're here."

"How do you know? Have you been able to visit the site? Do you have any idea if they're changing it so radically it won't even look like your fair? What if they decide to do something outrageous that will damage your reputation?"

A cloud crossed his grandfather's face.

"What?" Sam asked. "What's happened?"

"Nothing."

"Then why did you suddenly look unhappy?"

Gramps pushed a lock of white hair back from his forehead. "I'm worried about the direction Maxine wants to take the rodeo." He sounded fretful.

"How does she want to change the rodeo?"

After her great-grandfather explained, Chelsea laughed. "I like it! Camels racing instead of men beating bulls with spurs and cattle prods? I *love* it."

"You would," Sam said. "You've always liked weird, quirky things. The question is will that bring in money?

The answer, I can pretty well guarantee, will be a resounding no."

"Life isn't always about making money."

"True, Chelsea, but this is. The women are saying they need this money to save their town. Ergo, they need a real rodeo, not a weak facsimile one."

"Your dad has a point," Gramps said. "We need a serious rodeo. I have the same concerns. Camel races could be a fun thing on the side, but as a main attraction, it won't bring in attendees." He rubbed his chin. "Setting that issue aside, everything else is going well."

"But you don't know that. You can't get out there."

"I could if someone would take me." He stared at Sam.

"I'm not supposed to even know you, let alone take you out to the fairgrounds."

"It would blow your cover." Gramps humphed. "Guess you'll have to be my eyes and ears. But," he concluded, "don't be obvious in your spying on those girls. Just tell me how the place looks."

"It looks awesome." Chelsea leaned forward and threw her arm across his shoulders.

The older man's eyes lit up and he turned to Chelsea. "You've seen it?"

"Yeah, remember we told you we stopped on our way here yesterday?"

Gramps's face crumpled. He didn't respond. Sam worried.

"You should see the carousel." Chelsea tried to gloss over the moment. "It looks amazing."

"The women said Rachel did a great job refinishing it and fixing the engine."

"*Rachel* did that?" Sam stared at his grandfather. Motherly, nurturing Rachel didn't look tough enough to do all of that work.

"Yep. Scraped off layers of old peeling paint, sanded and repainted."

"I knew I liked her." Chelsea grinned.

"She fixed the engine, too?" Sam asked.

"Yep. A woman of many talents."

"Wow," Chelsea said. "I'm going to ask her to show me some of that stuff."

"You should, missy. She sets a good example for young women. You can do anything if you put your mind to it."

Gramps stood and heaved himself onto his bed. He lay back but adjusted the bed so he could sit up. "Every one of those women is a good role model. Each one has overcome obstacles in her life."

"Dad likes Vy," Chelsea blurted.

Sam cursed under his breath.

Gramps laughed. "Do you, now? Can't say that I blame you."

"I find her attractive but I don't like her. She's bossy."

"She's a strong woman," Chelsea argued. "As Gramps says, I should have strong role models."

Under his breath, Sam said, "Anyone but her." He needed more respect from his daughter, not less.

Sam had nothing more to say to Gramps about the fair. Obviously, his mind wasn't strong enough to deal with those women on his own.

"Do you want to play cards?" Sam asked.

His grandfather brightened. "Sure, what did you have in mind? Three-card stud?"

Sam shot him a critical look. "There's a young teenager in the room. We're not playing poker."

"Why not?"

"I'm not teaching her to gamble."

"We'll use pennies, for God's sake. It won't corrupt her."

"No. We'll play twenty-one, but no betting."

Gramps shrugged. "Okay."

Sam pulled a new deck out of his pocket.

They played on the dining tray, Gramps sitting up in bed, Chelsea perched cross-legged beside him and Sam sitting on the walker.

Before Sam knew it, an hour had passed. It had been like this when Gramps had visited at Christmas when Sam was younger.

While they played, Gramps regaled them with jokes, real groaners, and stories about his youth and the way the fair used to be.

Sam had never minded not seeing his friends over the holidays because his grandfather had been so entertaining. Now it looked like Chelsea was as sucked in by him as Sam had always been.

They left reluctantly, but Sam had to get back for the delivery of the cattle on Travis's ranch.

His stomach churned. Sure, he knew how to ride a horse, but he'd never done it in these kinds of circumstances...

Chapter Six

Useless.

Sam Michaels was absolutely useless as a cowboy.

Cattle teemed around him. He should be directing the herd, but it felt more like the herd was directing him.

The horse he rode refused to take orders from him. He could ride, damn it! He'd grown up riding every weekend, but Travis had put him on a stubborn, headstrong horse.

Where this horse and cattle were concerned, he'd earned not a speck of respect.

"What's wrong with this horse?" he shouted to Travis.

"Stubborn."

Yeah, Sam already knew *that*.

Travis ended up steering most of the cattle out of the yard and out to his fields. Sam could only follow and hector a few strays back to join the rest.

Dust swirled around him and dried out his throat.

The worst part? The other half of the herd would arrive on Monday and he would have to suffer this humiliation all over again.

Could he possibly have come up with a dumber idea for infiltrating the town? His impulse had been misguided from the start. He wasn't a stupid guy, but he'd thought his jobs would be things like mending fences, not moving a couple hundred cattle to a far-off pasture.

On the other hand, becoming a cowboy had been a last-ditch idea. He hadn't planned to use it unless he got desperate but Chelsea had screwed that up.

Back at the house, he and Travis sat on the back-porch steps and gulped down a couple of cold beers that Rachel had handed them. Sam wiped his face and the back of his neck with a damp cotton handkerchief she had also brought out.

Even at the end of March, this kind of hard work got a man sweating. The day's earlier drizzling rain had dried up. Light streamed across the land in nearly horizontal rays as the sun made its way toward the horizon.

Beside him, Travis cleared his throat.

In his easy, quiet way, he asked, "You want to tell me what's going on?"

Sam didn't pretend to misunderstand the question. He'd worked hard to fake it this afternoon, but had failed spectacularly.

In response to Travis's question, he said, "I wish I could. I really do. I guess you figured out I'm not a cowboy."

Travis didn't grace that ridiculous observation with an answer. He went straight to "What are you, really?"

"Until the end of last year, a successful businessman in New York. I got divorced and my wife and her father bought me out of our company as part of the settlement."

"So that part of your story is true. That's tough. You lost your livelihood."

"Don't feel sorry for me, Travis. I came out of it with a lot of money. My ex didn't screw me over financially. She just didn't want to work with me anymore."

"If you don't need the money, if you're not desperate enough to do this for spare cash—" he gestured toward the backyard, where the ground had been churned up by hundreds of hooves "—then why are you doing it?"

"Again, I wish I could tell you, but—" Sam scrubbed the back of his neck and grimaced. He liked this man and he liked his family.

It killed Sam that he betrayed Travis's open generosity with lies.

After a long swig of beer, he said, "I'm not a dishonest man, but I'm here under unusual circumstances. Would it be enough to assure that I would never hurt you or your family?"

Doubt arced through him. Would he hurt the family? If he ever learned that Rachel had ripped off his grandfather, Sam would prosecute to the full extent of the law.

Then again, if she were being dishonest with Gramps, she would deserve whatever happened to her, wouldn't she?

"I only got to this town before Christmas," Travis said, "but already this family, Rachel and her two girls, are the most precious people on earth to me."

He turned and stared a hole through Sam. "They are my family now. I would do anything to protect them. Give me one good reason why I should let a lying stranger stay in my home."

Tension radiated from Travis.

Sam was a good man, damn it, but how could he convince Travis of that when he'd arrived here under false pretenses? "I could give you a whole list of references who would vouch for my character if that would help. I can't do much more than that, though. It's complicated."

He bit down on frustration of his own making. He hated this subterfuge with a kind, generous couple.

Were they honest?

Until he could figure out for certain what the women were up to, he couldn't expose his purpose here.

His instinct told him Rachel was as honest as the day was long, as Gramps used to say, but Gramps himself questioned the women and their motives. And he'd known them for years!

"Travis, I won't charge a cent for the work I do here on the ranch, as imperfect as it is. I wouldn't dream of taking your money. I'll work for free."

Deceiving this man who'd given him a job felt like a terrible betrayal of Travis's decency. Decency had been a rare commodity in the men Sam dealt with on Wall Street.

"Would you like me to leave the house?" Sam asked. "I can go to a hotel."

Travis opened his mouth, but a squeal interrupted him, followed by the slamming of the back door.

They started and shot up.

Tori ran toward them and launched herself into Travis's arms. He caught her with one arm, not spilling a drop of his beer.

Impressive.

"Look! Travis, look!" she squeaked.

Travis's expression softened. No doubt about it. His love ran deep.

Travis blinked hard and hugged Tori until she complained, "You haves to stop holding me so tight, Travis. I gots to show you something."

"Sure," he said, easing up on the hug. "What do I have to see?"

Tori held out her hands. Hot-pink nail polish sparkled on her tiny fingernails. "Look what Chels did. It sparkles!"

"Those are beautiful nails." Travis held one small hand and admired the color. "You like Chelsea, don't you?"

"I *love* Chels. She's my bestest friend ever!" She wriggled to be put down. "I have to go. Chels is going to show me how to draw a pony."

When the door slammed behind her after she ran back into the house, it echoed across the empty yard.

"Well," Travis said. "I guess that settles it. Tori would be devastated if I asked Chelsea to leave now. You'll be staying. But…" Travis held up one finger.

Sam held his breath.

"I'm taking you at your word that you're trustworthy, but if you hurt my family in any way, I'll break every bone in your body."

Travis stalked into the house, leaving Sam in the slowly encroaching darkness to contemplate the irony that he was protecting his own family but could never share that with his host.

Sam hoped like hell that Rachel was innocent. He didn't want to face Travis if Sam had to have Rachel arrested or charged.

BECAUSE MOST PEOPLE went to Honey's for their Saturday-night entertainment, Violet closed up the Summertime Diner early.

At six, she trudged upstairs to shower and change. Rachel had invited her to dinner.

She didn't realize until she had put on her favorite dress and reapplied her makeup with extra care that she was primping for the new man in town.

She scowled.

She didn't care what he thought of her.

She didn't.

Nonetheless, she checked the dark seams on the backs of her stockings and adjusted one of the clips on her garter belt.

She smoothed the satin of her dark green-and-black polka-dot dress down over her hips and thighs. Large black vintage buttons she'd found on an old sweater held the snug bodice closed. One smaller, matching black button closed each cap sleeve to form a tiny pleat.

Snagging a black shrug from the bed, she put it on while she rushed to the front door of the apartment. She stepped into black suede pumps and glanced into the mirror beside the door, checking that she'd applied her mascara, eyeliner and lipstick perfectly.

She'd started building her style soon after coming to Rodeo to live with her aunt at sixteen.

Aunt Belinda had put her to work in the diner right away, only part-time, but Vy had felt compelled to contribute as much as possible for her aunt's kindness in taking her in. Every day after school and through every weekend, Vy worked. Trying to keep up with homework as well just about killed her.

Unable to manage both for long, she left high school and went to work for her aunt full-time. Aunt Belinda complained, but it had been Vy's choice. It had made sense at the time. Now, as an adult, the shame of the lack of her education burned through her.

The side effect of not attending school, however, meant that she'd developed her style in her own unique way.

As a teenager, she'd been crazy about old movies and, without the influence of her peers, had started wearing vintage clothing instead of the latest trends.

After her aunt died and left the diner to her, she'd revamped the menu and the decor to suit her style. Now not one customer or fellow citizen batted an eye at her choice of clothing.

But what did the new man in town think? With his sophisticated manners, he must find her... What was the word? *Gauche.*

In the car, knowing that she headed to the ranch with a chip on her shoulder, she tried to calm her burgeoning sense of outrage.

Cool your jets, Vy. This is a problem of your making, not his.

Good advice, but she struggled.

By the time she arrived, she was a nervous wreck.

Her partial salvation came in the form of a small ball of energy that rocketed against her legs. Vy picked up Tori and swung her around.

"How's my favorite girl?"

"Vy, look what I gots on my fingers!"

"Hot-pink! I love it!"

"With sparkles!"

"I can see that." Vy shot a smile toward the teenager hovering in the background. "Is this your handiwork?"

Chelsea nodded.

"I like it. Great color."

Chelsea returned her smile.

"Can you bring the two pies I brought into the kitchen? I don't want to let go of Little Miss Sparkles here."

She blew raspberries against Tori's neck, producing giggles galore in both of them.

Chelsea took the pies from the table where Vy had set them. Entering the kitchen, Vy wrapped her free arm around Rachel's shoulders.

"How are you doing, hon? Can I help you with anything?"

"I'm good," Rachel said. "Most everything is ready for dinner. What kind of pies did you bring?"

"A lemon meringue and a pumpkin. I had to use canned filling for the latter."

"Knowing you, you jazzed it up so it's special."

"It is," Vy admitted without a hint of modesty. She knew food well and how to prepare it. Or how to get her staff to make it great.

Chelsea took Tori with her out to the living room. It

seemed that, while she might have turned the corner into adolescence, her inner little girl wasn't quite ready to grow up. She seemed to enjoy Tori's lively spirit.

Vy leaned on the counter on her elbows while she plopped her chin onto her fists. "So?"

"So what?"

"So how is he doing?"

"Not well at all. Travis passed through a minute ago to head upstairs for his shower. He didn't look happy. I don't know what's going on. I'll find out later when we have some privacy, after everyone heads to bed."

For the first time, Vy doubted her wisdom in setting this up. She'd wanted to give the guy his comeuppance, but not at Travis's expense. "Maybe I shouldn't have sent him here. I'm sorry."

"I'm not. Tori adores Chelsea. I still say that if a man can raise a daughter that well, he can't be all bad. I don't know why he's here, but I'm giving him the benefit of the doubt."

"But can he even ride a horse?"

"I peeked out back a number of times. He wasn't doing well, but he managed to stay on the horse."

Vy laughed.

A noise in the kitchen doorway drew Vy's attention. She glanced back over her shoulder.

Sam stared at her with hot eyes, at the way her bottom thrust out because she leaned on the counter.

As she straightened, blood rushed up her neck and into her cheeks. Her fingers tingled.

She might be only thirty with a healthy sex drive, but it had been a long time since she'd felt this high a level of sexual awareness and desire. In fact, she couldn't remember it ever being this strong before.

Except that he didn't look like a fake cowboy tonight.

He looked real sweaty, dusty and dirty, as though he'd just come home after a long trail ride.

His hair lay flattened against his head and his thick socks belling out at the toes gave him a hint of vulnerability. The overall look made him more masculine, exactly what Vy didn't need him to be.

His jeans, no longer freshly ironed, creased in interesting spots and hugged thighs that were surprisingly well muscled.

If he wasn't a cowboy, how had he come by his body? He did something physical regularly. What? Gym workouts?

Does it matter, Vy? He's hot and he's the last man you need to be attracted to. He's dangerous to your peace of mind...and to what you thought was your contented libido.

He brushed past her to put an empty beer can into the recycle box, his heat sending out whiffs of hard-earned sweat.

She frowned. She dealt with working men all day long in her diner—ranchers and cowboys.

She hadn't felt this way about a single one of those men, trapped in the middle of a tug-of-war. At opposite ends were common sense and impractical urges, reason and insanity, objective thought and badly timed, inconvenient lust.

Sam backed out of the room, his easy flattery seeming to have deserted him.

Rattled, Vy went to the fridge to pour herself a glass of iced tea. "Do you want some?" she asked.

When Rachel didn't respond, Vy turned to find her watching Vy with an odd expression.

"I've never seen you look at a man like that before."

"Like what?"

"Like you want to devour him."

No. Vy drank down half of the glass of tea.

"Why is this man affecting you so strongly?"

"He isn't." Oh, but he was.

Vy watched Rachel try to tamp down her skepticism. "You've had a strong reaction to him since he stepped into your diner."

"How do you know?"

"Have you ever in the past called a local rancher to ask them to hire a cowboy you didn't know? Particularly a *phony* one?"

When Rachel put it like that, Vy had to laugh and opt for honesty.

"No. I haven't."

"So what is it about Sam?"

Vy stared out of the kitchen window above the sink to Travis's land beyond, not quite taking in the darkening landscape. "I don't know, Rachel. I can't figure that out."

"You always know your own mind, Vy. How unusual for you not to. Maybe that's what's really bothering you."

Vy refused to look at that. Tired on Saturday night, she steered away from introspection. Her head and feet hurt. She took off only one full day a week, Mondays and a half day on Sundays. Tonight she craved peace.

"I'll go set the table." She headed for the dining room, away from Rachel's probing gaze.

When they sat down to dinner, Tori claimed the seat beside her for her new friend, Chelsea.

With Travis at one end and Rachel at the other, Vy had no choice but to take the chair beside Sam.

His scent surrounded her, not cologne but a very subtle and, unless she missed her guess, expensive soap.

She'd never had the chance to flirt with a man like Sam. She'd never been able to dream of a better romantic outcome than her lousy life experience had allowed her.

But then, it hadn't been this kind of man who'd come sniffing around her mother's trailer, had it? If it had been, her life might have turned out differently.

But would he have treated her any better than Ray had?

We've established for certain that he's dishonest, remember? He's every bit as bad as Ray.

No, Vy, stop. That's an unfair comparison. Sam might be a pretend cowboy but he isn't Ray.

Her instinct reassured her that he was a better man. Even so, until she learned more about why he pretended to be a cowboy, Vy would not put one ounce of trust in his character.

She turned her attention to the two girls on the other side of the table, Chelsea giggling as though she hadn't already passed into what looked to be the beginning of a rocky adolescence.

When Sam reached for the salad, his elbow brushed Vy's arm. Adrenaline shuddered through her. She managed to hold back a gasp, barely.

He held out the bowl to her and she took it, careful to not touch him.

The house was charming and most of the rooms sized generously, but not the dining room. It felt close and hot, even though Vy knew that the actual temperature in the room sat in a comfortable range.

Yet the hot-and-bothered feeling, generated internally by her desire for a man she barely knew, turned her inside out.

Aware of every move Sam made and itchy that she noticed, Vy lashed out. "How did the roundup go today?"

She addressed the question to the table at large, but her glance shot to Sam, making it obvious who she was really asking.

When Sam didn't respond, Travis said, "Great. It was all great."

Travis made a good peacekeeper, but recklessness gripped Vy.

"How about you, Sam? How was it for you?"

"You can guess, can't you?" Sam's voice came across hard-edged in the softly lit room. "You already know how it went, don't you?"

The fake smile she offered him obviously made him angry, but he made her aware of longings she couldn't afford to feel.

"Oh, I can guess, all right, and I'm guessing it wasn't *great* at all."

Both Rachel and Travis frowned. She should keep quiet but forged on.

"I'm guessing you were a failure."

"Yes, I was," Sam said, voice sharp enough to cut the steak on his plate. "And that's exactly the result you hoped for when you sent me here, isn't it?"

"Yes," she hissed. "You came into our town pretending to be something you aren't."

"Vy." Rachel's warning tone barely broke through the haze this man evoked in her, anger, desire, anger, desire, with everything muddled inside her.

"With your lily-white cowboy hat and your smooth hands that have never been roughened by a single day's hard work in your life, why did you come here? To steal from us?" She didn't know why she was saying such stupid things. They had nothing worth stealing, but she was thrashing around in the confusing darkness of her own emotions. "Did you come here to make fools of us?"

"No!"

"Then why pretend to be something you're not?"

"I have my reasons, damn it, and they're none of your business!"

His booming statement echoed through the room, followed by the slide of Travis's chair across the bare floor as he stood.

"Calm down. Both of you. Right now."

Vy breathed hard. Her chest hurt. Her right arm ached from holding it close to her body so she wouldn't touch the man beside her.

Beside her, Sam's breathing pumped harshly in and out.

A tiny hiccup from the other side of the table caught her attention, Tori starting to cry.

Oh, dear freaking damnation, what had she done?

"Tori, no. Don't cry. Sweetie, stop. I'm sorry."

But the floodgates opened and Tori wailed, "Don't... fight."

Vy shot out of her seat and rounded the table, pulling Tori into her arms. Taking her to the sofa in the living room, she sat down with her in her lap and rocked her.

Since the day of her birth, Tori had been Vy's favorite child in town. She loved them all, but Tori had been her best friend's first. She held a special place in Vy's heart, and Vy had just hurt her, all because she was a loud-mouthed fool.

For ages, she whispered love and pretty sweet nothings to Tori until she calmed.

Chelsea hovered in the arched opening between the dining and living rooms, glancing between her father and Tori, clearly torn and not at all grown-up yet.

Vy nodded to her, set Tori on her feet and nudged her toward the girl.

Chelsea picked her up and deposited her back onto her chair.

Vy hovered in the archway and said, "I'm sorry for ruining your evening. I'll leave now."

"Vy, that's not necessary," Rachel said, expression stricken.

"Aw, Vy…" Travis took a step toward her.

"No." Sam stood. "These are your friends. You stay. I'll go."

"I said I'm leaving and I'm leaving." At home, she would pour herself a stiff drink and try to forget this man and her ridiculous, hot, unreasonable reaction to him.

"I insist that you stay."

"Don't you dare *insist* anything. You're not my boss." Vy pulled on her coat and picked up her purse.

From the dining room, she heard Rachel start to laugh. "Travis, they're fighting over who should leave, for Pete's sake. I swear those two would fight about anything."

As Vy opened the door to step out, Rachel called, "Vy, thank you for the pies. Sam, I'll bring a piece to your bedroom when I serve dessert."

Her wits gone and her equilibrium frayed, Vy drove home exhausted…and all because she'd sat beside a man for dinner.

She'd never been affected like this before. Never.

In the chilly darkness, she analyzed, trying to make sense of her attraction to bring it under control and kill it as ruthlessly as it needed to be excised.

After Ray, she'd kept herself under a strict set of rules about who she dated and how close she would let any man come.

How to understand her reaction to Sam?

Sure, he was good-looking, but so were a lot of the local cowboys. But there just wasn't a spark with any of them.

Why did Sam ignite not only a spark, but a furiously raging wildfire?

Vy let herself into her apartment and poured that much-needed drink.

Infernal, tempting man.

She took a cooling shower, then crawled under her heavy duvet, shivering.

Sleep eluded her for most of the night and she woke up early for Sunday morning's breakfast service, crabby and not at all ready for her day.

Chapter Seven

Sam drove into town for breakfast to give himself time alone with his daughter and to give Travis time alone with his family. Somehow it seemed right to give them a few hours of privacy on Sunday morning.

Silent on the drive in, he went over everything that had been said at last night's dinner table.

"Chelsea?"

"Yeah?" She stared out the window.

"I'm sorry for my behavior last night. It was bad."

"Why are you so untrusting of these people?"

"It's that one-dollar lease. It's the lack of a contract." He sighed. "It's my worry for Gramps."

"Why were you *so* angry with Vy? You treat Rachel nicely."

"Violet gets under my skin, I guess."

"I've never seen that before."

True. He wasn't that kind of man. He treated people with respect.

Wise enough to know that part of his anger had been fueled by the truth in everything Violet had said, he knew he shouldn't be here under false circumstances. But in his eyes, family trumped all.

Also, he could admit to himself that his pure unadulterated lust for Violet made him surly.

When he'd walked into the kitchen to the sight of her beautiful—

He couldn't go there. His desire for her made him behave like an adolescent in his cravings and frustration.

God, he needed to get over himself. He wasn't a randy teenager.

He laughed.

"What are you laughing about?" Chelsea watched him with a frown.

He glanced at her and at the sunny landscape on the other side of the passenger window. For the next few hours, subterfuge could take a flying leap. He could just spend time with his daughter as himself.

His latent good humor reasserted itself.

His mom used to say he was the most forgiving guy on earth and that it was impossible for him to hold a grudge.

That might have been true in the past, but these days, he sure held a grudge against Tiffany. She had chosen an indecent, difficult way to end their marriage.

Success is the best revenge.

True, but today he had time with his daughter on a spectacular Sunday morning and a little girl named Tori had mellowed Chelsea's 'tude somewhat.

"It's a beautiful day," he said, "and I'm riding into town to have breakfast with a beautiful girl."

"Feeble, Dad," she said, but humor lurked in her tone and it made him feel good.

As he and Chelsea entered the diner and found a table near the back, they continued a running argument about flirtation between the sexes, started when Chelsea had ordered him in the car to not flirt with Violet today.

"Dad, when you flirt it's your lizard brain talking, not your refined, reasonable man brain. Stop flirting. It's embarrassing."

"We're all hardwired to find each other attractive. It's what we do."

Violet approached. Sam smiled. She scowled. He sighed. She hadn't gotten over last night.

"What can I get for you?" she asked, the question was appropriate but her tone not so much.

Chelsea ordered and then he did, too. Without a backward glance, she left the table.

Sam frowned.

He loved laughter and silly jokes. Not cut out for espionage, this tension made the whole screwed-up situation hard on him.

"What I want to know," Chelsea said, "is *why* you have to flirt? Why not skip the games and just get to know each other?"

"Because it's hard to do that. When you start from scratch, you can't just sit down as strangers with a notebook and a list of questions and say, 'Okay, tell me who you are, what you like to do and what you expect from a relationship,' as though you can put it all into a computer and find your ideal mate. I know about online dating and that it works for some people, but it doesn't suit me. I like to play. I like the games. So I break the ice. I flirt. Flirtation is fun."

"But—"

"How else do you think the species propagates?"

"What about love?"

"I tried that once. Remember? It didn't work out so well."

After being quiet for so long Sam thought she'd dropped the conversation, Chelsea eventually said, "So you did love Mom when you married her?"

"Yes. I thought it was love, anyway. I was young. I bought into my culture wholeheartedly. Your mother went to all of the right schools. She came from money. We had the same conservative views." Sam sipped his coffee. "It didn't do us a heck of a lot of good, did it?"

Glumly, Chelsea said, "You got *me* out of the marriage, Dad. Aren't I worth something?"

He dropped his cup onto his saucer with a clatter, sloshing coffee over the rim. Grasping Chelsea's hands in his, he said, "You are *everything*. You are worth every single speck of heartache I went through with the divorce. I don't regret a moment of the marriage, because it produced you."

"Really?" Her voice cracked. She looked so hopeful. Surely she knew how much he loved her?

"I love you with all of my heart."

"I love you, too, Dad." Flustered by how deep and heavy the conversation had become, she gave him a tiny smile. "But *not* your lizard brain and your weak flirtations."

"Hey, I'm a free agent these days. I get to have fun and flirt all I want."

Chelsea rolled her eyes.

"Leave my lizard brain alone," Sam said. "It appreciates the beauty of the woman who's about to deliver our pancakes."

"After last night, she still looks furious."

"Yeah, she does, but I find it strangely appealing. It makes her eyes flash purple."

Chelsea rolled her eyes. Sam took out the change purse.

"Rolling eyes."

Chelsea dropped a quarter into the purse. "Just don't say anything dumb."

Sam watched Violet approach. "Man, she has great calves."

A second later, Violet plopped their meals onto their table.

"Chelsea, are you looking forward to watching Travis's

herd grow?" Sam asked loudly. "Don't you think it would be cool to watch calves being born?"

Chelsea kicked him under the table.

"Thank you, Vy, that will be all," Chelsea said, dismissing her with a spot-on imitation of her mother at her most snobbish. The girl should be an actress.

Violet frowned and walked away.

"Don't you think you were rude?" Sam asked.

"Are you kidding? I didn't know what was going to come out of your mouth next."

"Oh, ye of little faith."

"Oh, me of justified cynicism."

Sam nodded in positive assessment. "That's a sophisticated line for a thirteen-year-old."

Chelsea grinned. "I'm smart, you know."

Sam, in blessed harmony with her, smiled warmly. "Yeah, I know, possum."

"Let's make a deal," Chelsea said, still with a smile on her face. "You keep making me put change into the dumb purse. How about if every time I think your flirtation is dumb, you have to add a quarter."

Sam thought about it. Feeling expansive at the moment, he said, "Okay. You're on. Fair is fair."

Chelsea's happy smile looked good on her. Sam responded in kind.

He was still smiling when Violet brought their bill. He reached for it. Someone from another table had snagged Violet's attention so she hadn't yet let go of the bill.

Their hands collided. He jumped as though stung. She did the same. There hadn't been any sort of static electricity. Violet hadn't just walked across a carpet in the middle of winter, but Sam had felt electrified.

Good Lord, what was wrong with the two of them?

Vy ARRIVED AT the ranch on Sunday afternoon because Rachel had called her.

"You need to smooth things over with Sam," her friend said when Vy stepped into the kitchen.

"No *way*." She'd slept poorly and Sam had waltzed into her diner in a good mood this morning.

"Do you know he was actually *smiling* when he came to the Summertime this morning?"

"People do enjoy coming to your diner, you know. Maybe he was putting on a good face for his daughter."

"Nope. He was making comments that made his daughter smile, but that I didn't understand at all. They weren't even fighting this morning. I think he was making fun of me. He seemed to be in a genuinely good mood."

"And you aren't, so you need to criticize him."

"Whose side are you on, Rachel?"

"Believe it or not, yours. But Sam seems to be able to shake things off. You don't. You need to get over whatever is going on with this man."

If only Vy could wave a wand and all of her ridiculous sexual attraction to Sam would be gone. "You make me sound unlikable."

Rachel reacted quickly, reaching to hug her. "You are opinionated and tough, but you are *so* likable. Never doubt that, Vy." Rachel pulled back. "In this situation you, the Queen of Common Sense and Good Behavior, aren't behaving rationally at all. Examine that."

She was afraid to.

"Sam's in the barn doing chores. Go out there and fix this situation," Rachel ordered. "He lives in my house and you are my friend. I don't need this tension around me. I don't need you two fighting in front of my daughters."

Guilt kicked in, whether Rachel wanted guilt or not. Vy

knew she had to rise above her feelings and at least try to get over her attraction—and thus her bad mood—to Sam.

She trudged out to the barn and stepped inside.

It smelled faintly of manure but also of warm horse-flesh. Almost comforting and not altogether a bad scent, it calmed Vy. Somewhat.

Dust motes danced in a sunbeam streaming in from a high crack in the ceiling. The sunbeam landed on Sam's handsome head, setting off the highlights in his blond hair, as if he was the prize at the end of the rainbow.

When unwelcome desire shot through her, her resistance shot up. Thinking of Rachel, she cautioned herself to relax.

She could relate to this man without her emotions getting strung up like a bunch of Christmas lights.

She stepped down the aisle.

He glanced her way. His hand stalled. The horse huffed out a breath and Sam resumed his brushing.

"You don't look like you belong in a barn."

"Neither do you," she retorted.

"My boots are covered in crap, my clothes are dusty and my hat's sweaty. I belong here a whole lot more than you do." He glanced her way. "What brings you out here? Come to make fun again?"

"No." She gathered her courage. She wasn't a woman who apologized easily. "I'm sorry I behaved so badly last night."

"Why did you?"

"Did I what?"

"Behave badly."

Like she would ever admit to him that she found him attractive. "I was tired. I work long days, you know."

"Yeah. I can guess. Let's not kid each other, though. That had nothing to do with it."

Vy's breath backed up in her throat. "What do you mean?"

"You weren't put out because you were tired." He tossed the brush to the floor. "You weren't *angry* with me." He hauled off his leather gloves. "You were upset because of this."

Before she realized his intention, he grasped the back of her neck and pulled her close. His mouth descended on hers, harsh and hard and taking a lot more than she wanted to give.

Or than she *thought* she wanted to give.

She gave, all right, igniting in fury and desire. And then she gave more, as much as he demanded of her.

When a fire burst inside her, she angled his head so she could take from him. And take.

And he gave. And gave.

Breathing roughly, they pulled apart. Vy stared at the new man in town. His gray eyes, not the least bit cool, dared her to complain that he'd taken control.

Nope. No complaints. Not a one. She liked it.

She'd been the one in control for too many years, through every incident, every problem, feeding the town during snowstorms, blackouts, ice storms and every other emergency that befell Rodeo.

Being the town go-to for solving problems had exhausted her. She hadn't realized how much.

Her body leaned toward him for the relief of abdicating control to someone else, even if only briefly.

Bad idea, Vy. But she allowed it, just for these few precious moments.

His heat along the length of her body curdled her insides and turned her knees to jelly. He didn't feel soft. His body didn't feel unused. Who was this man, this non-

cowboy, who was no pushover no matter how much she
wanted him to be?

"Mmm," he said, kissing her neck. "Fried onions. My
favorite aphrodisiac."

She laughed and tried to push him away, but he held
on, and maybe she hadn't pushed very hard.

"Now that we've acknowledged our attraction to each
other," he said, "do you want to tell me why you hate me
so much?"

His warm breath, coffee-scented and sweet, ruffled the
small hairs around her face.

"You're a phony. You're no more a cowboy than I am."
Funny that she criticized him, even while she still held him
against her with her arms around his neck. Funny that she
tightened her grip so he wouldn't move away. Funny that
he didn't seem to take offense to her words.

"Considering how obvious it is that I can't even fake it,
well, yeah. I am not a real cowboy, but I have my reasons."

His nearness and heat, his height, his insightful gray
eyes disconcerted her.

People came to her for her cool head under pressure.
She needed to reestablish her independence.

She pushed away from him harder and he let her go,
her latent defenses kicking in at last, as they should have
done before he'd kissed her.

But, oh, she'd wanted that kiss. That spectacular kiss.

"Does Travis know you're not a real cowboy?"

He snorted. "What do you think?"

Then he did the oddest thing. After frowning, he took
a small, glittery purse out of one pocket. He unzipped it
and rummaged in his other pocket until he came up with
a quarter, which he dropped into the purse. He put the
thing back into his pocket, all without seeming to realize
what he'd done.

"What was that about?"

"What?" he asked.

"That." She pointed to his pocket.

He glanced at his crotch and back at her, as if checking to make sure he didn't have a hard-on or that his zipper wasn't open.

She rolled her eyes. "Not that. *That.*"

He grinned sheepishly. "It's something between Chelsea and me. I got tired of her attitude on the drive out here. Her snorting, indignant teenage huffing and puffing and her eye-rolling bothered me so I make her pay a quarter every time. Not that she really snorts but it's for any rude noise she makes. Or that I make."

"On your drive out from where?"

He opened his mouth, closed it and appraised her with an approving eye. "Good one. Nice try. Do you know what the most useless word in the English language is right now?"

"No. What?"

"D'oh."

"There's no need for sarcasm. I don't know. Okay?"

He smiled. "No. I mean the word *d'oh.*"

She smiled, too.

This strange, unprecedented harmony with him ruffled her feathers so she rushed to change the subject.

"Why are you here?"

His expression flattened. "That's private."

"Why won't you tell me?"

"Can't."

"You are the most frustrating man. How can I trust you if you won't confide in me?"

He actually looked pained. "I just can't. Okay? It's private. Don't ask again."

"Okay, but in that case, no more kissing. No more man-handling."

"Is that what I was doing? Manhandling you? You participated in that kiss willingly." He tucked her hair behind her ear. His touch thrilled her. "It was great, wasn't it?"

She spun away from him. Yes, she had participated and it had been wonderful.

But she'd made one doozy of a mistake once with an untrustworthy man and wouldn't do it again.

"I need to get home."

She stomped out of the stable and straight to her car without entering the house.

As much as she loved Rachel, Vy couldn't see her right now, not after that kiss and how much might still be showing in her expression, like desire, temptation and need.

Sam Michaels crept closer and closer. She shouldn't allow it. It ended now. Today.

She'd been kissed many times before. Sam's kiss wasn't anything special.

Well, yeah, it was. That kiss had sent her spiraling in a whirlwind of sexual need.

Damn. This called for another cold shower to rein in her unruly, rowdy desire.

SAM SHOULDN'T HAVE kissed her. He cursed his lack of self-discipline.

It had been amazing, though.

The woman was passionate with a capital *P*, all locked up tightly inside her as though *passion* was a dirty word. Maybe kissing her hadn't been a bad thing.

What if they started an affair? With that kiss as an example, Violet must be fantastic in bed.

And then what, Sam?

Combing Storm roughly, which the horse seemed to like,

Sam caught himself. Having an affair with Violet was nothing more than fantasy with a good dose of wishful thinking thrown in, and utterly unrealistic considering that he investigated her as part of the fair committee.

Another impediment loomed and that was Violet's character. There was more to her than he had first thought. She might be ripping off his grandfather. On the other hand, she might not be.

She sure had the respect of the community.

Despite the animosity between them, he wouldn't do anything to hurt her. He wasn't a man who used women, and she didn't deserve to be used.

Her self-control impressed him or would have if it didn't also thwart him from getting to know her better.

But he had a life to return to in New York. He stepped out of the barn and headed for the back door for a cold drink.

No, he wouldn't use Violet in that way, but remembering that kiss, he wished he could.

AFTER BREAKFAST ON Monday morning, Sam headed out to the stable to saddle Storm. The second half of the cattle shipment should arrive at any minute. The horse might love being brushed, but he hated being ridden.

Sam was fit. In New York, he boxed most nights after work at the local gym. He rode his horse every weekend. He and his friends participated in amateur polo events.

But he couldn't ride this damn horse he'd been saddled with. Not well, anyway.

The devil waited for him patiently in the barn. After a couple of aborted attempts, Sam managed to get the horse saddled. He got himself up into the saddle and rode out of the barn.

The shipment arrived moments later.

Again, in a deeply aggravating déjà vu of Saturday's debacle, both the horse and the cattle made a mockery of his attempts at authority.

When he returned to the yard sooner than he'd intended because Storm decided he should, laughter from the back porch provoked him. When he recognized the laughter as Violet's, his temper shot through the stratosphere.

She stood with her hands on her hips, her teeth a broad slash framed by red lips, watching him attempt to control Storm.

She was laughing at Sam yet again. It maddened him.

He forced the horse around and advanced on her.

He boiled. He fumed.

He took action.

Chapter Eight

Vy's laughter faltered.

Sam had heard her. Fury crossed his features.

He rode toward the porch.

Her stupid unruly laughter, self-defense against her attraction to this man, had gotten her into trouble again. He forced the horse close to the porch.

Vy shrieked and stepped back, but with nowhere to go because Rachel stood behind her.

"Rachel, move," she said.

"I don't think I will." What was that smugness in Rachel's voice about? "I want to see what Sam has in mind. You shouldn't have laughed."

"You're supposed to be my friend."

"I am, but I asked you to straighten all of this out yesterday. Somehow you didn't. Today you're laughing at him again. You need to take resp—"

Vy never heard the end of Rachel's comment. Sam grasped her around her waist and hauled her up onto the horse without breaking a sweat.

Outraged, she shouted, "What do you think you're doing?"

He didn't answer, features hard as he rode across the yard and away out into a field…and kept going.

She grasped his jacket, her position precarious. She started to slip and wrapped her arms around him.

He held her against him securely, not a cowboy and not a rancher, yet he as strong as one. Still he rode, until they were well out of sight of the house.

Why did this look so romantic in movies? Her butt hurt. The ride jarred. Her teeth knocked together.

He stopped beside a tree and wrapped the reins around one gloved hand. With his teeth, he tore off the other glove and clasped his long fingers across the back of her neck.

His kiss—*oh, my Lord*—it smoldered and burned and singed. If yesterday's had been electrifying, today's was even more potent. Again with the giving and taking and taking and giving nonstop for minutes on end, stupefying and intoxicating.

More. More.

Her head spun. He stepped down from the horse and took her with him.

He whirled around, setting her back against a tree.

The kiss held. She tasted him, welcomed his tongue and gave her own to his mouth.

She plundered and plundered.

His hands pushed up her skirt, pulled aside her panties and grasped her behind, his touch on her skin thrilling. *More!* Running on instinct, she wrapped her legs around his waist, still kissing him, drinking equal parts anger, determination and passion.

She didn't want this. She craved it. She held his head so she could feast.

No other man had…

"Do you want me, Vy?"

"Yes. Now!"

He entered her.

Fulfillment spread from her core to the tips of her fingers and toes.

Yes. This.

There were moments in life, pivotal moments, when everything changed. Like right here. Right now.

No. She couldn't accept that. Couldn't—

Sam moved inside her, giving her life, brightening dark corners, loosing inhibitions.

She'd been cold for so long.

Still that kiss went on and on.

She wasn't a taker, though.

Vy Summer gave as good as she got.

Infusing every caress of her fingers on his body with fire, she set to turning Sam's insides to jelly to match hers.

He moved with intensity. She met every stroke.

Two hard bands of muscles, his arms across her back, protected her from the rough bark of the tree. Dappled sunlight played across her closed eyelids. An elusive, fresh scent teased her. Sam's soap.

Intensity built. She clung to his shoulders. Desire crumbled Vy's last remaining defenses and she fell into a chasm of delight.

Sam followed.

For long moments, Vy reveled in the aftershocks, holding him against her as hard as her arms could.

Don't leave. Don't be over. Not yet.

Let me float here in this oasis of delight for just a few more minutes.

Sunlight still played hide-and-seek with her eyelids, warm one moment, cool the next.

Sam held their bodies locked together, not one fraction of space between them. She couldn't remember ever being with a man and feeling this close after sex.

But then, that hadn't been just sex. It had been…

She didn't have words for it. Stumped, she leaned her head forward and placed the sweetest of kisses on his neck.

Most times, she didn't have the patience for cuddling after sex. She liked to get it done and leave, but right now she could drift in this spectacular state of joy for ages.

Sam pulled back. She opened her eyes. He studied her with affection, his gray eyes dark in the shade of the tree.

At some point, he'd lost his hat. Vy rested a tender hand on his hair.

She wasn't prone to tenderness, but Sam's childlike delight in corny jokes and his acute love for his daughter and his… She didn't exactly know what it was about this man…

But he made love superbly.

When she was with him, so did she.

An unsteady grin spread across his handsome face. "I'm glad we got that out of the way. Now, Miss Retro Diner Owner, are you going to laugh at my riding skills again?"

Mercurial man, trying to make light of a situation that had taken them both by surprise. Vy had just made love against a tree in the middle of the day on her friend's land…with a relative stranger. And she didn't want it to end.

And Sam seemed as shaken as she felt, even though he tried to joke.

She kept her affairs discreet, an expression of normal physical needs and nothing more.

That, what she and Sam had just done, had definitely been something more. So much more.

The *more* worried her. Sex was fine and dandy. More was not.

Fear arose in her. Panic. No. She didn't want more. She wanted safe platonic affairs with a little physical loving on the side. That was *it*. Pain, so much pain, threatened in the *more*.

Only at this moment did she realize Sam had controlled his troublesome horse and had ridden with skill across the field to the edge of the stream, all while Vy had had no doubt that he wouldn't let her fall.

She could no longer laugh. She could no longer use his clumsiness to keep her distance.

Angered by his skill, the very skill she'd moments before thought nonexistent, she pushed against his chest. More sturdy muscle there, like on his arms.

"What do you do?" she asked, annoyed that he was more than he seemed.

"About what?"

"How do you keep in shape?"

One corner of his mouth tipped up. He knew that it bothered her when he broke through her negative assumptions about him. "I box almost every night. Back home."

"And where is back home?"

The other corner of his mouth quirked up. "I've told you, that's private."

He lifted her from his body and set her down gently, holding her hand to make sure she landed on her feet.

His consideration, second nature to him, puzzled her and robbed her of fodder for her anger.

Okay, he seemed to be a good guy in certain ways.

And she had wanted him. Had craved his touch.

She stalked to the edge of the stream and struggled to push through her bewilderment to find her equilibrium. Her sense of normalcy.

Like a person who'd received a shock, she couldn't find her feet.

"What are we going to do about our attraction to each other?"

"No!"

"What?" he asked.

"I won't be attracted to you."

"Too late, Violet."

"I refuse to be attracted to you. I can control myself. Can you?"

"Usually." He smiled ruefully.

Neither of them had been controlled.

What a ridiculously messy situation.

"I live in this town." To her horror, tears trembled in her voice. What on earth? What did this man bring out that she didn't want to show? "You're passing through. I don't know why you're here. I don't know why you're pretending to be something you aren't, but any havoc you wreak in town will mean nothing to you because you can walk away. I can't. I love this place. I want to live my whole life here. After you leave, I'll be left behind to pick up the pieces. Understand?"

"Yes. I do." He sounded reasonable, and maybe sad. She turned to look at him. His expression open and honest, he said, "I didn't mean for this to happen."

"Neither did I. Now that it has, let's put it behind us. It won't happen again."

Now for sure, he looked sad. "It was amazing," he said.

"It was okay."

Seeing through her, he laughed, but she couldn't give their lovemaking credence. She couldn't let him know how much he'd just shattered her world.

She tried to mount the horse, who, surprisingly, hadn't run away.

Storm sidled in the opposite direction.

Sam grasped his reins. Storm tried to resist. Sam said, "Settle down!"

The horse behaved like the most docile pony in the barn. Wonder of wonders. Sam had won the fight.

He mounted the horse, then reached down for her.

Again they rode across the fields, but slowly this time.

"I need to get home." The same thing she'd said yesterday after he'd kissed her, as though all of her problems would be solved if she could just get to her small apartment, crawl into her bed and cover her head with her blankets.

When she'd come here today, she couldn't have known she'd be having sex with Sam.

She'd wanted it, and had dreaded losing herself to him, and had thought it would never happen. But losing herself had been magnificent.

It had been great, amazing, disturbing. And tender. And affectionate.

When they returned to the house, Vy left without a word or backward glance.

Sam Michaels might be an enigma, but she liked him, and that made him more dangerous than ever.

Sam watched Violet walk away, taking a piece of him with her. Their lovemaking had been nothing short of dazzling.

For a man his age, he hadn't had many lovers. He'd lost his virginity in high school, had fun in college with a handful of partners and then had gotten married soon after graduating and getting his first job.

For the fifteen years his marriage had lasted, he'd been faithful. Then about eighteen months ago, Tiffany had told him it was over and that she was marrying her new partner the second the divorce papers were signed.

There'd been no one since then, no matter how great the temptation. They'd all looked like rebound love, and he hadn't wanted that.

But today's lovemaking with Violet had taken him to unprecedented heights.

For that brief period, he'd been lost to himself and everything around him, as though transcending time and place. He'd been at peace for the first time in a long time.

He wanted more of that bliss. That ecstasy.

Which was why, he thought as he put Storm away and trudged to the house to wash up, he would stay away from Violet.

He should never, ever depend on a woman to complete himself. He had to be on his guard. Tiffany had taught him that. It would probably be years before he would trust a woman again.

Violet, powerful, beautiful and funny, had too much sway over him. If he gave her power and she betrayed him, the effect would be even worse than it had been with Tiff. Ironic, given that he'd known the woman only four days.

Only four days and already she had him riding off into the sunset with her and making blissful love to her up against a tree.

And in the afterglow of that amazing experience, he realized his only course of action, to protect himself, was to stay far away from Violet.

After washing up in the downstairs washroom, he entered the kitchen.

Rachel stood at the counter, chopping vegetables. He should offer to help her but needed to be alone, to still the tremors of shock running through him and to regain his equilibrium.

She glanced at him over her shoulder and must have seen something on his face, even though he'd thought he looked neutral.

"Vy just hightailed it out of here without saying goodbye. You look like you've just survived an earthquake."

Earthquake. Good word for it.

"You want to tell me what's going on?"

Sam shook his head. He really couldn't talk about it. He'd never been the type to kiss and tell, especially not with something too huge, too important to sully with gossip.

He turned to leave the kitchen, but Rachel stopped him with a hand on his arm. "Just don't hurt her. She's been through a lot in her life and she's a good friend. I won't see her toyed with."

Sam covered her hand with his briefly, and then lifted it from his arm. "Rachel, I'm very much afraid all of the hurting is going to go the other way."

As he stepped out of the kitchen, he knew Violet could damage him in ways he never could have expected.

He hadn't imagined the glory of that kind of lovemaking existed. Oh, yes. She could hurt him. Big-time. Without even trying.

And, as much as he feared for himself, all of his instincts screamed for him to protect Violet.

He'd developed a wellspring of tenderness for prickly Violet Summer.

Sam vowed to stay away from her. He'd find a way to help Gramps while crossing paths with her as little as possible.

Vy awoke with a start.

Disoriented, she stared around the room. Not her bedroom. Yes, hers. Nothing looked the same.

Everything had changed.

Life felt different.

She felt different.

In a fog, she rolled over. Light had not yet started to creep past the curtains. Still early on Tuesday morning or the middle of the night. She wasn't late for work. So what was wrong? What had happened?

In a rush, it came roaring back, flooding her with fury and passion.

Sam Michaels had happened.

She sat up and cradled her head in her hands.

No way. One bout of lovemaking with a man didn't change her. Didn't make life feel grand and new and... bigger.

How had she allowed Sam to happen? She never lost her restraint. Her sexual experiences with men were mutually satisfying and easily abandoned.

She chose her rare encounters carefully, with those men who wanted nothing more after sex with her than "Thank you, ma'am" and "See you around." Pleasing but easily forgotten.

Not so Sam. In a few short days, he'd gotten under her skin. Into her blood. Madness. Temporary insanity. Or maybe not temporary. Her body had been branded by his touch. By him having been there. Having touched her.

Having been touched, she couldn't be untouched by him. She would know him with her eyes closed, with the caress of a single finger.

Crazy.

No one got to her like this.

Tossing back the covers, she surged out of bed for the shower.

She'd taken one the night before but needed another immediately, not because she felt dirtied by what they'd done together but because she *didn't*.

He'd singed her. Had impressed his mark on her.

It had been astounding, the best sex ever in her life... yet only a quick tumble against a tree. How could that be the best ever? Because of Sam, a man she didn't trust.

She opened the curtains fully. Off in the distance, a vague promise of dawn colored the horizon, too far-off to be a reality for an hour or more.

Even in the darkness, the world sparkled through her new wide-open eyes. Sparkled!

No.

This wasn't her. Her head couldn't be turned so easily.

Smart, level-headed, sensible—these were the words that defined Violet Summer, not *moony, infatuated* and *sparkly.*

She'd spent years creating a persona, the person she really wanted to be, all the while hoping that nobody would call her out for the imposter she feared she was. Uneducated Vy.

She wanted to be smart Vy.

Sam called her Violet, a name too soft, too vulnerable and too... In her past, all her mother had ever called her.

She showered, dressed and left her apartment to trudge downstairs and open her diner.

Stepping inside, she struggled to become Vy again, bold, clever, successful businesswoman.

She was just full of adjectives for herself today...and all of them that she'd wanted to be ever since leaving home at sixteen. She'd forced herself to become strong, to become a thesaurus of sass.

Blinking in the harsh lights of the kitchen, she gathered ingredients for the pies she made every morning.

From the quiet kitchen, amid the rattle of baking pans and measuring spoons, Vy heard the front door open.

She didn't panic. It would be Will, and part of a familiar routine. They'd been doing it for years. Maybe all of this would settle her nerves.

She heard Will walk through the dining room to hang his coat in the spare room at the back.

He stepped into the kitchen. "Hey."

Will wasn't much of a conversationalist.

"Hey, yourself. I'm making six apples and a couple of cherries."

"Okay."

"You can get started on the meat loaf and beef stew."

"Same as every morning."

"Get the potatoes on to boil. Put plenty of garlic in the oven to roast. The garlic mashed potatoes have been popular lately. When I'm finished with these pies, I'll open up."

"All the same as every morning." Will sounded puzzled.

"It's wet out there. Probably be busy early. People will want lots of warming comfort food."

Silence. No movement.

Vy glanced at her cook. He stared at her, his expression as inscrutable as ever. Überhandsome, thirtysomething Will had a string of women in town circling around him but as far as Vy knew, he didn't partake of offers. Just kept his reticent distance. The man didn't give anything away— Vy didn't even know where he'd come from—but he was a stellar cook and dependable, so he could remain as taciturn and solitary as he wanted for all Vy cared.

"You okay?" he asked.

"Of course. Why wouldn't I be?"

"Don't know why, but you're chatty. I've known you a dozen years or more. You aren't *ever* chatty."

And here she'd thought she was sounding normal.

"You're kind of bright today, Vy. Do you have a fever?"

Yeah, she had a fever all right, and its name was Sam.

Caught between despair and hysterical laughter, *sparkly*, life-affirming laughter, she put together her pies, planted them in the ovens and opened the front door.

At six, customers wandered in. By six thirty, the joint was jumping and Vy was glad of it. Hard work took some of the sparkle out of her. She settled into her normal routine. If it lacked luster, so what?

She had no time in her life to be giggly lovesick. She had no room for a man who rode into town claiming to be something he wasn't.

What if he had come into her diner and said simply, "Hi, I'm Sam and I like the way you look, I like your laugh, I like your jokes, will you go out with me?"

But no. He'd come here in disguise. With only one previous kiss, without one single date and without a declaration of caring or affection, he'd taken her against a tree.

But, oh, that taking had been astonishing.

Besides, she'd taken him right back.

Honesty compelled her to take a step away from faulty thought, from her assumption that she would have dated him if he'd come to her in a straightforward fashion. She knew better. Where affairs of the heart were concerned, she was a coward.

With good reason.

There were only so many things she deserved in this life. Amazing sex wasn't one of them.

"Vy?" Lester Voile watched her silently from his seat. "That coffee's gonna get too cold to drink if you don't start pouring soon."

Vy stared at the coffeepot in her hand. She had no memory of picking it up and walking to Lester's table. She had no idea how long she'd stood there woolgathering.

What she did know was that her cheeks were hot with memories of yesterday. Here she stood like a fool, thinking about what she was consciously to walking away from, instead of doing her job.

She pulled up her proverbial socks, or in her case stockings, and squared her shoulders. Vy, diner owner extraordinaire, took over.

"You're absolutely right, Lester. This coffee won't get served on its own." She filled his cup, patted his shoulder and got on with her unsparkly day.

Right here, this diner? These people? This was it. This was all that she deserved. They were good people, in a good town. She lived a good life. She had more than she could have ever hoped to gain in her lifetime.

Suck it up, Vy.

Be grateful for the life you have and move on, even if it means accepting less.

What *less*? Sure, she'd had mind-blowing sex with Sam, but that was all it was. Just sex.

A squiggly, squishy, warm part of her mind protested. She'd felt more. Had he?

But he wasn't honest, was he? He was a pretender. She knew too much about those. He could have pretended his warmth for her. He could have pretended his guilt about being here falsely.

He could have told her the truth about why he was here. But he hadn't.

Case closed.

No more lovemaking. No more joking, sarcasm or giving him a hard time in her diner. No more Sam. He would be just another customer. That was all.

Only he wasn't.

He didn't return to her diner.

Chapter Nine

Chelsea and Sam visited his grandfather every other day. Sam had missed his doctor a number of times because of work. They'd played a frustrating amount of phone tag.

Every time they saw Gramps, he reiterated that he didn't know exactly what felt wrong about the fairground deal. He only had a hunch, an instinct that not everything was on the up-and-up and that Sam needed to dig deeper.

Sam objected, "I don't know what else I can do without raising suspicions."

Gramps leaned back in his chair. "How is Vy doing?"

Sam shrugged. "Haven't seen her lately."

"Aw. That's a damned shame. I like Vy's spark. She's got great 'tude." He glanced at Chelsea with a twinkle in his eye.

She giggled.

"Gramps, you suspect these women might be cheating you and yet whenever you speak of them as individuals, you sound admiring. I'm getting mixed messages."

"Um…"

"Gramps?"

He looked so confused that Sam backed off. Now that he could clearly see the state of Gramps's mind, he wondered whether the women might be honest after all.

But what about leasing for a dollar and taking over

Gramps's house and not signing an agreement regarding profits?

"You're not helping out much by being so vague," Sam said.

"Sorry." Gramps rubbed his hands together. No, not *rubbed*. More like washing them, but without soap and water.

Sam left Gramps's room frustrated and confounded. He didn't have a clue how to find out any more about what was going on other than to call Samantha Read and demand that she show him the books.

And he couldn't do that. If he played his hand so plainly, Vy would never talk to him again. Her opinion had become important to him, more important than it should be.

Climbing into his vehicle, he asked himself, *what's my next step?*

He had no idea.

OVER THE NEXT two weeks, while Sam herded cows, mucked out stalls, mended fences and in general helped out around the ranch, he became comfortable with his role as a cowboy.

He liked the work. He liked how physical and honest it was, and how uncomplicated, after dealing for so long with volatile markets or equally volatile personalities or overweening greed.

Travis and he developed an easy relationship working together. If not for Gramps's problem, he might have relaxed.

As well, if there weren't so many calls and texts from New York about the new business, he might have been able to move faster in his investigations. Between working on the ranch, visiting Gramps and fielding criticism from his new business partners about being out West, he struggled to find time to question people.

Sam wrestled with the issue of his grandfather's dilemma while his time limit in Rodeo became shorter and shorter. He'd asked everyone around town what they knew about the fair as casually as he could.

To do any more would raise suspicions.

He became more and more worried about his grandfather. Gramps's mind wandered, had holes and bumped along from one topic to another. He told the same stories about the past over and over. He pulled out his wallet and counted his few bills repeatedly, sometimes only minutes apart. Not that he needed money in the home, but he seemed to need reassurance that he had money, even a paltry hundred dollars important to him.

At last, Sam and his grandfather's doctor, who visited the home a couple of days a week, met up. Yes, these were symptoms of dementia creeping in.

Was dementia behind Gramps's original worry about the women? Was the committee innocent of wrongdoing and had Sam been wrongheaded in his approach to the women and this town?

Should he have come here honestly?

He decided the time had come to look at the problem from a different angle, and to interview one of the women on the committee, someone to whom he'd not had exposure yet.

He chose to talk to Honey Armstrong, the woman who owned the bar at the edge of town. It would be easy enough to talk to her by just going in and ordering a drink.

According to Rachel, who he'd asked about the members of the committee, Honey had a good head on her shoulders.

Nadine, as a journalist who wrote for the local paper, might find his curiosity too suspicious. Sam didn't want anything he said to become fodder for an article, so he ruled her out.

Apparently, Maxine was a good woman but had a chip on her shoulder the size of Montana. Sam didn't need complications. Just answers.

He figured he'd pumped Rachel for answers enough that he couldn't bother her more.

A drizzly Saturday afternoon found him leaving Chelsea to visit with Gramps while he occupied a stool at the bar, where he ordered a beer.

He hadn't seen Violet since that day beside the stream. He'd avoided the diner. He missed the food.

Get real, Sam. You miss her.

How could that be? He barely knew her.

"You're Sam, aren't you?" Honey was a knockout. Miles of curly blond hair ran down her back. Deep-set china-doll blue eyes watched him steadily, the intelligence in them sharp.

"Sam Michaels. I take it you're Honey?" He held out his hand to shake hers.

With a smile that could shine through a hurricane, she took it.

"You're one of the women working on that fair outside town?"

She nodded.

"Looks like a big job. The rides are shaping up. My daughter wants to be first in line for the carousel."

"It's beautiful, isn't it? You're staying with Rachel. Did she tell you that ride was her baby? She's the one who restored it."

"She did an amazing job." He drank some of his beer. It was midafternoon and the bar was quiet. She didn't seem inclined to end the conversation, so he figured he might as well jump in.

"How did this whole process come about? How did you all decide to do this? I mean, it must have been a daunting task to take on."

She was off and running about everything they were doing, everything except how the finances worked, which made sense. He was, after all, a stranger.

"I heard the park had gone to seed? The owner was happy with you reviving it?"

"Carson Carmichael. Yep. He supports us completely." While the words might sound positive, something flickered across her face, here and gone almost before he caught it. Discomfort or worry?

Interesting. "So will he get any of the profits once the fair is successful?"

She chewed on her lip. "*If* it's successful. This is a real leap of faith we're taking, hoping that people are nostalgic for something that was a fixture here for the past hundred years."

While she lost herself in thought polishing beer glasses, Sam asked, "How certain are you that people will come out?"

"We're not. Not at all." She rallied and smiled. "Of course they will. Effort pays off, right? We're all working our butts off, so it has to be a success."

He hadn't gotten around to the question of how much they were leasing the land for, because he didn't know how to do it without seeming suspicious. He made a terrible detective.

It wasn't until after he'd left that he realized she hadn't answered all of his questions directly. Would Gramps share in any of the profits?

That "if it was successful" implied as much, but Honey hadn't answered the questions directly so Sam didn't know.

Damn.

What now?

He drove past the amusement park on his way toward town to head back to Travis's place. He pulled up onto the shoulder and got out to stare at the house in the distance.

Again, a wave of longing passed through him. He still had no idea what it represented. Why was that house so important to him? Sure the fair should have been his legacy, but he'd never cared enough to come out to claim it, had he?

In a week he would head back to New York and his new business, to salvage the pride that Tiffany and her father had trampled during the divorce.

Success is the best revenge.

He would never choose to give up his life in New York and his career to live here on the amusement park land. So why this draw? Why this constant feeling that he was missing something? Or missing out on it?

Nothing more than a solid brick two-story vertical rectangle, and nothing a fraction as beautiful about it as the house he owned, still it drew him.

He couldn't get inside.

And yet...

He wanted to check it out, to stand inside it just one time. He might get away with asking for a tour of the grounds to check out the fair, but he could come up with no reason to ask to see the house.

Why had the women wanted it as part of the fair lease? What was in there? Were they hiding something?

There's only one way to find out, he thought as he pounded the side of his fist on the top rung of the fence.

He would get inside on his own.

Tonight.

Vy STARED AT the pregnancy test.

Only two days late, but for a woman whose body worked liked clockwork and had for years, this was cause for concern. Hence, the home pregnancy test she'd driven to the next town to purchase.

No sense getting the rumor mill going.

Besides, she knew the symptoms.

She knew her body well. She recognized the changes, even so early, sixteen days after that afternoon with Sam.

With breasts tender and sore for no good reason, and nausea threatening every morning, she knew.

Oh, dear God, she knew.

They'd been rash. They'd had sex without protection. Vy had been so upset about giving in to temptation that she hadn't given the possibility of conception a second thought.

Shame on her.

After using the test, all vestiges of doubt washed away.

She was pregnant.

She would go to the doctor for a blood test, but she knew.

What on earth would she do now?

Her life about to change permanently, she buried her head in her hands as though she could escape the truth.

But there was no escaping the reality. A baby, a precious child, grew inside her.

A terrible fury roared through her. She wouldn't give up this child. She *couldn't* give it up.

On the other hand, she couldn't let Sam into her life. He hung around town working for Travis, but still he refused to state his true intentions.

Or so she assumed. She hadn't had a conversation with him, but Rachel would have passed along anything she'd learned.

She couldn't trust him. Yet one thing her conscience compelled her to do was to be honest with the man.

For the remainder of the morning, she fretted, another new experience for Vy. Ordinarily, she didn't sparkle and she certainly didn't fret. She dealt with problems head-on, skipping the worrying part altogether.

Huge and bringing back too many memories, not all of them good, this new wrinkle colored every action and every step she took.

Her heart ached. Her stomach burned.

That afternoon, she told Sam.

"ARE YOU SURE?" Sam stared at her with his mouth open. It would be funny if this wasn't a laughing matter.

"Positive. I haven't seen a doctor yet, but I used a pregnancy test and I know my body."

He staggered against the stall door and leaned on it. Vy had shown up on the ranch so she could break the news in person.

"Whew! I didn't expect this."

No, he couldn't have. "We're a pair of adults," she said, "who had sex without once thinking of birth control. We didn't use a condom. Shame on both of us."

"I guess I assumed you were on birth control."

"You didn't ask. Did you seriously assume?"

"No," he admitted. "I didn't give it a single thought."

"Neither did I."

He scrubbed his hands over his face.

"I guess I didn't think at all."

"We were worse than a pair of high school students, heedless and…"

"And horny. You were angry. I was angry. We wanted each other. I've never wanted a woman like that before.

No excuse, I know, but what a mess. What now? What are your plans?"

Vy stilled. "What are *my* plans? We've just determined that we both made this baby."

"I'm saying that it's your body. You decide. Are you telling me you would agree to an abortion if I asked for one?"

"No!"

Again he scrubbed his face. "I didn't think you would, but I had to be sure. For the record, I'm not asking for that. Whew. This is unreal. I can't wrap my head around it."

"I assume you plan to go back to wherever it is you're from sometime soon?"

"New York City."

"What?"

"I'm from New York City and in one week, I'll be driving home to start a new company with two partners, a multimillion-dollar investment firm."

"Multimillion?"

"That's what I do. You know I'm not a cowboy. I'm not a rancher. I'm a businessman."

"So, Mr. Not-A-Cowboy-But-Really-Mr.-Businessman, what now?"

"I don't know. I'm having trouble breathing and assimilating this." He spun away but turned back. "You're sure?" he asked again.

"Reasonably certain."

He blew out a lungful of air. "Whew."

There'd been *more* in the lovemaking and Vy wanted *more* now. She realized what the more looked like for her. A vehemently independent woman at all times, right now she wanted comfort.

She wanted Sam to wrap his arms around her and tell her that everything would be all right.

But that didn't happen, and she didn't think it would anytime soon, judging by the shell shock on his face.

"I live in New York and you live in Montana." He shook his head, bewildered. "How can we work this out?"

"I won't live in New York and you won't live here."

"I can't stay here. I have to go back to New York. In a dozen days, my new company goes live."

"And you have to be there?"

"Yes."

"Why?"

"Because I have to. I have to make sure it's a success."

"Money is that important to you?"

"It isn't about the money."

That took her aback.

"It isn't? Then why start the company?"

"To prove a point to my ex-wife that she picked the wrong man to end our marriage for. He's not a fraction of the businessman I was. He's now running my old company."

He shot out a breath. "I want revenge for her betrayal. I plan to get it by starting a company that will be so successful she can't help but feel regret."

Okay, so the guy was hurting because of his ex-wife. How did he go from New York to Rodeo?

"Why are you here?"

He jammed his hands on his hips and hung his head. He didn't, or couldn't, meet her eye. "I can't tell you why."

When he met her gaze, his eyes were filled with regret. "I wish I could be the most honest man you've ever met."

"Me, too." Regrouping, pulling her broken heart together shard by shard, she asked, "What *can* you do for this baby?"

"I can give the baby a life of relative ease. A good education. The best nannies so you can still run the diner."

She had been right all along about him being wealthy.

"I assume you want to still run the diner," he said.

"Oh, yes. It's my life."

"So is my work in New York."

Stalemate.

"I'm tempted to tell you what you can do with your money…"

His jaw tightened. "Don't. You'll need it. Take every single thing I offer you."

"How do you know I won't come to you with constant demands, to bleed you dry?" She was pushing him, yes. Her tone hinted of anger and maybe desperation. She'd hoped for so much more than this business arrangement.

"We could draw up contracts."

Contracts. Worse and worse. Not only was there no *more* in this conversation, there was a whole lot of *less*.

And her heart broke a little more.

Bitter and chagrined, she turned to walk away. "Your lawyer can talk to my lawyer."

"We don't need lawyers. You don't trust me?"

"I've had precious little reason to trust the people in my life in the past. And you haven't exactly been forthcoming, have you?"

He nodded. "I'll sign anything."

So. That was it. Disappointment thrummed through her. She'd given up thinking that any man had anything to offer her, but apparently, as she'd just learned, hope dies a hard death. A tiny corner of her had hoped Sam would come through.

So unreasonable, Vy, and so unrealistic.

But still she'd hoped.

Vy swept out of the stable to begin to make plans for the rest of her life with her child.

If she wanted to cry… If she felt like she'd just lost something huge…well, tough.

SAM LEANED AGAINST a stall door and slid down until his ass hit cold concrete, his heart beating like Mick Jagger prancing onstage during a sold-out show.

How had this happened?

Well, he knew *how* it happened, but how had the two of them, mature adults both, allowed themselves to get caught like this?

That afternoon, why hadn't one of them stopped for one precious second to say "Wait, do you have anything? Are you on the Pill?"

But there'd been no thought. Only action. Glorious, un-precedented…irresponsible action.

And now they'd created a little human being.

Holy crap.

They'd screwed up royally.

He'd never known so much desire in his life. Apparently, Violet had felt the same way.

Their lovemaking, their passion, the pure and utter coming together of—no, it was too melodramatic to say souls…but of their bodies—had been unlike anything he'd ever experienced.

But did he want to become a father again? Now?

Did he want to leave New York permanently to live in Montana?

No.

Absolutely not.

He had a plan.

He had a lot at stake back home.

Success is the best revenge. His mantra. His sanity.

Yeah, he needed success after the way Tiffany had betrayed and gutted him. The clock was ticking. He needed to get home.

Vy was pregnant.

What a disaster. Out-of-his-control life events just kept happening to him.

No, not *to* him. He'd brought this on himself. It was purely his fault. Like a randy boy, he'd made love to a woman without using a condom.

Yes, he'd been lost in the moment.

Yes, he'd been angry with Violet and it had inspired passion they'd both felt.

Yes, he'd wanted her more than he'd ever wanted a woman.

Not one of the above was a valid excuse for the poor actions he'd taken.

Their actions had created a child.

What a freaking mess. There was a baby.

How did he explain this to his daughter?

He guessed there was no time like the present. Feet heavy, he trudged toward the house.

Chelsea sat with Tori on the sofa reading a book.

"Chelsea," Sam said.

She glanced up, noticed his expression and sobered.

"Can we talk?" Even to his own ears, Sam's voice sounded unnatural.

"Sure, we can talk." She dropped the book onto the coffee table and stood.

Tori stood, as well. "I talk, too."

"No, Tori," Chelsea said. "I need to talk to my dad alone."

Sensing the tension and darkness radiating from Sam, Tori started to cry.

Sam called, "Rachel?"

She entered from the kitchen with Beth asleep in her arms.

"What's going on?"

"I need to talk to Chelsea alone for a few minutes. Tori is picking up on…um…tension."

"Okay. Tori, come sit with Beth and me." Rachel sat on the sofa and Tori tried to crawl onto her mother's lap. "Just a sec." Rachel put the baby down beside her and then hugged Tori.

Before leading Chelsea out to the backyard, Sam said, "When she goes down for a nap, you might want to consider phoning Violet. She's going to need a friend right now."

Rachel frowned but nodded.

In the backyard, sitting at a picnic table Travis had installed just a few days before, Chelsea said, "What is it, Dad? You're kind of scaring me."

"I don't know how to say it without just blurting it out."

She made a sound in her throat of impatience. "So, just blurt it out."

"Vy's pregnant."

Chelsea waited for more. "You have to give me more to go on, Dad. Is that good news for her or bad?"

"I don't honestly know. The part that affects you and me is that I'm the father."

Chelsea did a fair imitation of how Sam must have looked to Violet. Her mouth fell open and stayed open.

"How did it happen? I mean, I know *how*. Do *not* share any of that! I do not want to see those kinds of images of my dad! I mean, how could the two of you sleep together and not use birth control?" Agitated, she stood, walked away and then returned. He let her work through it.

"Wait a minute, *when* did it occur? How did you even freaking get together? You sleep in this house. Did Vy sneak in at night? How could the two of you have an affair in Rachel's house when she's been so nice to us?"

"Stop! We didn't sleep together here. There was never any sleeping around."

"Then when did it happen? And where?"

"It doesn't matter. Those are details a father doesn't share with his daughter."

Chelsea thought and thought. "You two barely know each other. How could you sleep together?"

"It happens."

Chelsea crossed her arms. "Well, it shouldn't. Aren't you supposed to be teaching me all about responsibility and safe sex?"

"Yes, I am."

"This kind of thing isn't an accident. It's because people are thoughtless."

"Violet and I behaved irresponsibly."

"A baby," Chelsea whispered and stared across the fields, trying to process what Sam had told her.

"Chelsea, I'm sorry. I screwed up."

"There was no thought of birth control."

Sam sighed. "That's correct. Neither of us thought of it."

"Not cool, Dad."

"Not cool at all."

"What now?"

"I'll send child support, of course."

Chelsea stared at him.

When he said no more, she yelled, "That's *all*?"

"What do you mean?"

"You're not going to raise her? Or him?"

"I've raised you. I've already raised my family. I'm a little old for starting over."

"Thirty-nine isn't ancient. It isn't too old to have children."

"You didn't seem to think I was that young when we first got here. You kept talking about how old I am."

"I was joking!"

"I'm not. I don't have time to start a new family. I have a huge new business to run. It's what's most important to me right now."

"Change what's important to you!"

Success is the best revenge pounded through his veins. He couldn't change it.

"What *you* want doesn't matter," Chelsea said, voice still raised but no longer shouting. "What's important is what the baby will want."

"How can we know what that is?" he asked.

"I don't know, Dad. A home. A solid family life. I had one until Mom decided she wanted to ruin it. Now everything is awful."

"Life isn't perfect. Every one of us has hardship in one way or another."

"Some more than others. Vy will be a wonderful mother. You've been a good dad. Until now."

She ran away. Sam watched her jump into his vehicle and slam the passenger door shut.

What the hell?

He shot off the picnic table, but his long legs got caught in the braces and he ended up on the grass on his back.

He swore pungently.

When had his life started to go so wrong?

Twenty months ago, everything had been fine. Normal. Predictable. Now he couldn't see from day to day what was going to crop up next.

He wished he could lie here all day long but he couldn't.

He sat up and walked to join Chelsea. Once inside the SUV, he asked, "Why are we here?"

"I want to go see Gramps."

"Why?"

"I don't know. I just want to see him."

He'd sprung a real doozy of a surprise on her. Driving her to see her great-grandfather was the least he could do.

At the nursing home, Chelsea ran into her great-grandfather's room well ahead of Sam. By the time he entered, he found Chelsea sitting on Gramps's lap, saying, "Vy's pregnant and it's all Dad's fault."

Gramps's white eyebrows shot to his white hairline. "Vy is pregnant?" He glared at Sam. "You did this to her?"

"I didn't *do* anything *to* her. *We* did something together."

"And seemed to forget everything your parents must have taught you about sex and contraception."

"In the heat of the moment, yes. We did forget."

Gramps smiled.

"Why are you doing that?" Chelsea demanded.

"Doing what?"

"Smiling at a time like this?"

"Children are special. They are always a blessing."

"Yeah, but—" Chelsea said. "Shouldn't people plan for them?"

"Yes. Yes, they should, but your dad didn't. A child is on the way and we will celebrate." He forced Chelsea's head away from his shoulder. "Chelsea, my dear favorite great-grandchild, can you do me a favor?"

"I'm your *only* great-grandchild."

"Not for long." Gramps's eyes sparkled brightly.

"What's the favor?"

"Please go to the front desk and tell Angela I have good news to celebrate. Ask her whether she can get someone from the kitchen to bring us three bowls of ice cream."

"But—"

"Please, dear."

"Okay." Chelsea left the room.

"How can you be happy about this, Gramps?"

Gramps frowned. "I love you, Sam. I like Vy. You two made a baby. It will be lovely."

"Lovely? It's a huge complication. I live in New York, remember?"

Gramps's happy expression fell.

"You won't stay here now that Vy is pregnant?"

"Gramps, I already told you. I have to leave for New York in one week. My partners have been more patient with me than I deserved. They've covered for me all over the place. If I don't return, they'll gut me."

"You said you got a lot of money from that company you sold to Tiffany's father."

"Yes, I made a bundle."

"So why do you have to start another company? Why not retire for a little while here in Rodeo until you figure out what you want to do next in your life?"

"I already know. I want to start this company."

"Why now? Why so soon after everything that happened with Tiffany?"

"To prove to her that she made a mistake."

Oh, crap, he hadn't meant to blurt that out. He hadn't meant to be so honest,

"You want to salvage your pride."

He might as well go all the way. "I want to make a hugely successful company and rub Tiff's and her father's noses in my success."

"Ah. Success and revenge."

Sam completed the thought. "Success is the best revenge. It's what's been keeping me going since all of this started."

Gramps nodded. "I understand."

"You do?"

"Sure, I do. It's a natural reaction. Wrongheaded but natural."

"Why wrongheaded? This I have to hear."

"Because bitterness and the need for revenge will eat away at your soul."

Sam didn't respond, his revenge was important to him.

"You could always stay here with Vy. Have a real strong marriage this time. A real love."

"What I had with my wife was real. At least for the first ten years or so."

"I guess."

Stunned, Sam paced the room.

"You guess? Gramps, there was a time when I loved Tiffany very much. If I'd never loved her, her betrayal wouldn't have hit so hard."

Carson sobered. "I can see that."

"Tiffany wasn't bad. She was just misguided. I didn't realize when I married her that the only things we had in common were shallow."

Carson nodded. "Like your backgrounds, your financial situation, your education."

Sam leaned back against the windowsill and crossed his arms and legs, settling into the knowledge that he'd been so wrong about himself and Tiffany. "All of those things. I guess I thought it all mattered. Plus, she was attractive. Unnaturally so. Doll-like. Perfect."

"And what do you think now?"

"There wasn't enough depth underneath the trappings. Tiffany wanted to live on the surface. She loved the money, the big house and the expensive clothing and jewelry. Even knowing it an illusion, she liked it. Then she began sleeping with someone else and blew all of *my* illusions out of the water."

"You never suspected."

Sam shook his head. "I thought of her as an honest woman. I've learned how truly little I knew about her."

"Happens to the best of us. How long would the marriage have lasted if she hadn't left you?"

"I don't know. I believed in honoring our vows. I would have worked my butt off to keep us together, at the very least for Chelsea's sake."

"So you were happy?"

Sam mulled that over before giving in to his innate honesty. "No. Not for a few years. I wanted more," he admitted. "I got some of that when we had our daughter but…you know, I had to work hard to convince Tiff to have even one child. She thought it would ruin her figure. She refused after the first pregnancy to do it again. I always wanted two or three."

"And soon you'll have another child."

Sam's gaze sharpened. "The timing couldn't be worse."

"Then you shouldn't have had unprotected sex."

Yes. True. "I'll pay her generous child support. The child will have the best education and nannies."

"I'm sure that will keep Vy warm at night."

"Vy made the same mistake I did."

"Yes. You both erred. Big-time."

"Gramps, I'm confused. I'm kind of scared. This isn't what I thought would be happening in my life." He turned to stare out the window, trying to take solace from the scenery beyond. "Violet and I would never make a successful couple even if I did think I could handle getting married again. We're too different. I'll do the best that I can for her, though."

"Do you understand that she truly deserves the best? I suspect Vy has had some harsh things happen to her in life and she guards her heart with a tough shell, but underneath, there's a truly loving woman."

Sam agreed. He'd seen her with Rachel's children. Tori

adored her. Despite her prickly, stubborn exterior, Violet loved people. She would be a good mother.

"Here's the thing, though, Gramps. I don't want any more children now. I wanted them when Chelsea was little. I've done my child rearing."

"What are you saying? That you won't get to know this child at all?"

"He's saying that *all* he's going to give Vy is child support." Chelsea had returned to the room from ordering ice cream.

"You won't even visit?"

Sam's stiff, uncoordinated nod elicited glares from both Gramps and Chelsea.

Unfair. Since arriving in this town, people had allied themselves against Sam. "What have I done to deserve all of this bad treatment? Huh?"

Chelsea opened her mouth but Sam cut her off. He pointed a finger at his grandfather. "You called crying about your problems here in Rodeo. These women were ripping you off. You needed help. I came running. *Running.* Do you know why?"

Gramps shook his head no.

"Because I love you. And what did I get?"

Again he shook his head.

"People blocking me at every turn. I've shoveled shit and ridden a demon horse and done hard physical labor for zero wages. Not one person has said thank you." He pointed at his daughter. "And you! Your mother took off on an adventure with her new husband. I stepped in to take care of you. I was ecstatic that she hadn't wanted full custody. I was overjoyed when she said you could live with me. I was hugely excited about taking a road trip with you. Do you know why?"

"Because you love me?" she whispered.

"Yes! What did I get in return?"

She shook her head.

"Attitude. I got *'tude*."

He whipped the small change purse out of his pocket and threw it onto the bed.

"Vy made me angry. She turned me inside out with her mouthiness and her sarcasm and her beauty. I desired her. Okay? I was lonely. I've been lonely for years." Until he said it, he didn't realize how true it was. "I was lonely. I wanted a woman. In particular, I wanted Violet. I gave in and took what I wanted. She was more than willing. One time I took what I wanted. One lousy time. What am I getting in return?"

They shook their heads.

"A baby I don't want!"

A nurse stepped into the room with a big smile and holding a tray with three bowls of ice cream.

Sam said, "Chelsea, I'll wait for you in the car. Take as long as you want. One of you eat my share."

With his anger spent and a resigned sigh, he left the room and the building. In the car, he wrenched his seat as far back as it would go and closed his eyes.

So much was his own fault and so much was outside his control. What was up? What was down? What was right or wrong?

He no longer knew.

Chapter Ten

Vy called her friends together for an emergency session at the diner. They snagged a table for six in the window.

Vy joined them with trepidation because she planned to come clean with them, about being pregnant, but also about why it raised so many emotions in her apart from joy.

Would they judge her as harshly for sleeping with Sam as her mother had for her teenage folly?

Thoughts of her mother brought on the great overwhelming sadness she'd buried years ago. Yes, she had done a solid job of submerging it in deep underwater chambers, but there'd been days, awful, come-out-of-nowhere, hitting-her-in-the-side-of-the-head days when her sadness would threaten to capsize her boat.

Violet, I'm so disappointed in you.

Could she survive someone she loved having such profound disappointment in her again?

Her friends waited patiently for her to explain the meaning of this emergency meeting.

She'd never been a coward, but she hated the thought of losing a single one of them.

"Talk to us," Honey ordered.

Come on, Vy. Suck it up and tell them the truth.

She opened her mouth and said quietly, "I got pregnant when I was fifteen."

After stunned silence, Honey said, "You have a child?"

"Somewhere, yes. I gave my baby up for adoption. I hope she's happy."

"Why do you look guilty?" Nadine asked. "Did you think we would disapprove?"

Vy nodded.

Max piped up with a vague hint of reproach. "I wasn't much older than that when I had my baby. None of you judged me. You could have shared, Vy."

"Why did you think it was so bad?" Nadine asked. "Why didn't you ever tell us? We wouldn't have thought badly of you."

Maybe yes, maybe no. "Because of the story behind it."

"Will you tell us? Please?" Rachel leaned forward, the frown on her face disturbing to Vy. What would she do without Rachel?

"My dad died when I was twelve," she plunged in, but her voice broke. She'd thought she'd done all of her grieving years ago, but here it was, choking her again. "I thought he was the best father on earth. He used to call me his little buddy. We did a lot together."

They waited patiently, all of them so smart, so wise, open receptacles for whatever she chose to share with them.

Today it had to be all of it.

"My mom and I lost everything. Dad had a life-insurance policy but it wasn't huge, and Mom didn't know how to get by in the world. Dad had taken care of everything for her.

"So she sold our house for the little equity they had in it for extra money. We moved away from our neighborhood where my school and all of my friends were, a neighborhood I really loved. We bought a small trailer."

Rachel nodded. Now she must understand Vy's problem

with trailer parks. Almost. She would think it was only
just because she'd lost her house, but no. It was so much
more than that. So much worse.

"We had money in the bank but Mom was terrified. She
said it would have to last for a long time. For her lifetime.

"Then a couple of years later, I guess she was lonely
and started seeing this guy. Within a couple of months, he
had moved in. It was already so crowded compared to our
old three-bedroom brick house. Now there was this man,
this virtual stranger, living with us.

"I really disliked him. On some deep level, I realized
that it was more than just adolescent angst that this man
was trying to take my father's place. There was something off about him that my mother didn't see. I recognized how sneaky and slimy he was. He was slick and, I
was sure, dishonest."

She gripped her hands. "It got worse. I disliked the way
he looked at me when Mom didn't notice."

Vy shivered in memory. A few nods around the table
in sympathy. They could all see where this was going.
Almost.

They had no idea how much worse it would be.

"Anyway, I thought he wanted Mom's nest egg that she
thought would sustain her for the rest of her life. I wanted
to prove to her how reprehensible he was. I arranged for
her to catch us in bed together."

A few gasps around the table. She hated that judgment
and rushed on.

"I wasn't actually going to go through with anything. I
still had my clothes on, but I definitely let him know that
I was reacting to the invitations he'd been putting out to
me. I didn't plan to let him go far because I knew to the
minute when Mom would get home, so I wouldn't have to
do anything too gross with him.

"Mom came home and caught us. My blouse was undone. He was on top of me. She cried and told him to get out and never come back and then she ran away. She was gone the whole night. I was so worried about her."

"What happened with the guy?" An ominous silence followed Maxine's question.

After a while of deep breathing, Vy said, "He was furious. He saw what I had done. He knocked me around."

Maxine winced. "He raped you, didn't he?"

Vy nodded. "He told me I deserved it for leading him on and for messing with the good thing hc had with my mother. I said, 'You've been looking at me the wrong way since you moved in.' I screamed and yelled at him. I was furious, too. It was an awful fight.

"He said I'd brought it all on myself by being a tease and a flirt. I had *never* teased him because I couldn't stand the sight of him. He said he saw the way I flirted with this guy who walked me home from school sometimes. I asked, 'What made you think I wanted anything to do with you? What gave you the right to ogle me with such disrespect?'

"He said if I was going to give it away for free to a young guy, I could just as easily give it to him, a real man. I never thought of sleeping with the boy. I just really liked him. We talked about books, for God's sake. We never even kissed."

Honey reached across the table and covered Vy's white-knuckled fists with her hands. "Stop blaming yourself. Stop justifying your actions. Even if you had kissed the guy, even if you'd gone further, it would have been your choice and it wouldn't have been wrong. It wouldn't have made you dirty or made it all right for another man to take anything from you."

Vy breathed out a little of her worry.

"Did he leave the trailer?" Max asked.

"Yes. That night."

"What happened with your mother?"

"She asked if I had led him on. I told her only that one time did I respond to *his* invitation, to reveal the snake he truly was. She was angry. She said hateful, hurtful things, that he would have never betrayed her if I hadn't led him on. I think she thought she would never find another man. In hindsight, I realize how scared she was, how afraid to be alone. She said she was kicking me out, that if I was so smart, I could go make my own way in the world."

Nadine covered her mouth with her hands. "And then you found out you were pregnant."

"Yeah. Mom let me stay until I gave birth and gave the baby up for adoption. Then she sent me here to Rodeo to live with Aunt Belinda."

"And your mom?" Honey asked.

"She hasn't spoken to me since. She's convinced that I orchestrated the entire thing, not to expose him, but to get the attention I was missing since my dad died."

"Was there any smidgen of truth in that?" Nadine asked.

"God, no. If I were going to do that, I would have chosen a better man to get attention from. My dad was a really good guy. My mom's boyfriend was not."

"Was it hard to give up the baby?" Max asked. Max had kept her child, but then, she'd had some support from her child's grandfather. They now lived on the ranch that Max had managed to purchase from him a couple of years ago. She was proud of her accomplishments, despite the heavy mortgage she carried.

"Yes, it was," Vy responded. "But I knew I was too young. I knew Mom was going to send me away. I knew I couldn't give the baby the advantages she deserved. I didn't want her to be held back by having a deadbeat father. If I could have, I would have erased him from her DNA altogether."

Vy stared at her hands. "I'm so glad I got to hold her once. I couldn't see even a trace of that man in her. I thought I saw a tiny bit of my dad. In her nose."

Her friends watched her silently.

A trembling smile touched her mouth. "Wishful thinking, I know. Now you know my whole sordid story."

Honey reached across the table and took her hands. "I'm sorry you didn't tell us sooner."

"So you could know how truly crazy I am?"

"So we could understand how incredibly strong you are." She swept her arm around the diner. "Look at the success you've made of yourself."

"My aunt willed me a diner. I got lucky."

Nadine added her two cents. "The diner was *not* like this when we were teenagers. It was ordinary. Normal. This is fun and current and busy because people love the food and the atmosphere, not because it's the only diner in town."

"My aunt made it a success."

With a vigorous shake of her head, Max said, "No. Your aunt started it and kept it going, but you've made it thrive. You're able to hire more waitstaff than your aunt ever did. You brought in an excellent cook. You updated the menu so people love eating here. People were tired of processed cheese on white bread and canned tomato soup."

"Remember what you said to Carson?" Rachel asked.

Vy cocked her head. "I've said a lot of things to Carson."

"About Lester. How he watches the Food Network and then comes in here asking you to make the recipes for him."

"Oh, yeah."

"So have you ever done it?"

"A couple of times. Remember the feta-and-watermelon salad last summer?"

Nadine hummed. "That was so good."

"Lester's idea." Vy turned her attention back to Rachel. "What is your point about that?"

"You listen to your customers. You took Lester's request and made it a reality. Lester comes to the diner because he lives alone and hates to cook, but also because you provide this awesome congenial atmosphere where he can socialize with his neighbors and get great food at good prices."

Vy smiled slowly. "Yeah, I guess I do well in that area."

"In every area," Max said. "Even if you are bossy and sarcastic at times."

"Most of the time," Nadine cut in.

"Your point being?" Vy asked, and they all laughed.

It felt good. A great, huge load had been lifted from Vy's shoulders and she felt not only lighter but also more at peace.

Except for…

"There's more news," she said. "There's a reason I had to tell you about my past."

"I wondered," Nadine, the consummate journalist and on the ball, murmured.

On a breath that gusted out of her with panic and dread, Vy said, "I'm pregnant."

Into the shocked silence that followed, Maxine asked, "Now?" followed by Nadine's "Who?"

"Sam Michaels," Rachel said. "That day he carried you off on the horse."

Vy nodded.

"Sam told me you'd need to talk. I've been on pins and needles since you called to ask us all to meet. Now I know why."

Honey stared at Vy with her big blue eyes. "Sam carried you off on a horse? And you made love with him?"

Vy nodded again.

"Except for the unintended consequences, I'm jealous. He's gorgeous."

"But not honest. Not a real cowboy."

"True, Vy."

Ever blunt, Max got down to brass tacks quickly. "What now?"

"Sam knows. I just told him."

Rachel held sleeping Beth in her arms. "Which is why he came into the house looking like he'd been struck by lightning and wanting to talk to his daughter."

"So he's told her. I wonder what Chelsea thinks. We were so irresponsible. We didn't give a single thought to birth control."

"What did Sam offer?" Max leaned forward. "What's he going to do for you and the baby?"

"He's going to pay child support. He said this baby will have the best of everything," Vy finished bitterly.

"But he won't stick around to help you raise the child?"

"No, Rachel. He won't. He's from New York City and has a business to run."

"I thought he was better than that." Rachel shook her head. "Have we figured out why he's here pretending to be a cowboy?"

"No idea," Vy said. "He didn't offer an explanation. He only said that he had to get back to his life in the city."

"So, this guy comes to town, takes advantage of a local girl and then skips out. I should cut off his balls."

"Maxine!" Nadine shouted, but then laughed. "Yeah, we all should."

"He used you," Maxine said, angry on Vy's behalf.

"To be honest, I used him, too."

"There was certainly plenty of lightning arcing between you two whenever you came out to the house, Vy, even if it did look like dislike."

"There was a powerful attraction, Rachel. True. I…I'm afraid I fell for him hard."

Max's lips thinned. She had a low opinion of men, with good reason.

"There will be a lot of talk around town," Vy said. "I'll understand if you want to stop being my friend."

Max swore harshly. "Stop that kind of stupid talk. We're not going to stop being your friend just because you experienced tragedy when you were young and then got pregnant again now." She glanced around the table. "Every one of us has something going on in her background. Not one of us is perfect. Maybe that's why we get along so well."

She gestured with a hand down her body, drawing attention to her masculine clothing. "You guys are all so beautiful, but you've never made me feel ugly or out of place or less than you. We stick together no matter what."

Vy glanced around the table. Everyone nodded.

These women. These wonderful, amazing, accepting women.

They'd met shortly after she'd been sent here as a teenager and had been a part of her life ever since.

"There's one more thing you might not have realized," she said.

"What is it?" Nadine asked. Nadine, with her college degree, might be the most judgmental of all of these women once she heard.

Vy pressed her hands onto her thighs. "I never finished high school. I don't have a diploma."

"Because of the baby and having to leave home?" Again, Nadine.

"Yeah, but also because I felt like I owed my aunt so much. What if I hadn't had anywhere to go when my mom kicked me out? Aunt Belinda was a lifesaver and she treated me well."

"I remember when we used to come in after school and you were serving our table," Rachel said. "At the time, I didn't think much of it. It was just part of reality, you know? But later, I wondered why you had never been in school."

"Somehow I fell through the cracks. I should have been there." She'd felt the lack ever since. "Maxine, you mentioned that we've never made you feel less than the rest of us because of your lack of femininity, but I've always felt less than all of you because of my lack of an education."

"Vy," Rachel said in a warning tone. She of all of the friends really understood Vy. "Do not for a single minute believe that you are not as good or worthy or smart as us, because that is utter nonsense."

Again with her reserved gesturing, Max indicated the diner and its customers. "My God, Vy, let's get back to this place. You've made this diner a success. You make food that's current yet homey. Add your own distinct, feisty character to the mix and this place rocks!"

"Yeah, my feisty, uneducated character."

"Don't do that." Max's sharp, fierce tone took Vy aback. "Don't turn away praise with sarcasm. You always do that. Most of the time it's funny, but today you need to own what we're saying. I'm the last person who should be telling you this, me with all of my weird neuroses, but accept our love, Vy. You deserve it. Okay?"

Deserve. That word Vy had so much trouble with, considering her actions when she was young.

Max reached across the table, took one of Vy's hands in her own and squeezed. "Okay?"

"Yes," Vy whispered. "Okay."

"Okay, what?" Max asked.

"Okay, I accept everyone's love and support. Thank you, damn you!"

That broke the tension. They laughed.

Overwhelmed by the goodness and affirmation, Violet stood. "I'd better get upstairs to pull myself together."

For a moment, she felt as lost as she had all of those years ago to find herself without her mother's support after the rape and then to find out she was pregnant by a man she despised.

But that was then and this was now. Now she had friends. Mind-blowing friends.

"I'm tired. I think I'll take a short nap."

"You know where we are." Honey picked up their coffee mugs. "I can help out here if you need to take time to deal with this. It's huge."

"Call if you need anything," Max said.

Everyone else agreed.

Chapter Eleven

Shortly after eleven, in pitch darkness, Sam crept onto the porch of his grandfather's house. No lights from within penetrated the moonless night. Thank goodness the women didn't waste money on electricity when no one was about.

A cool breeze cut through the denim jacket he wore. It ruffled his hair. He shivered.

He'd brought a flashlight and a credit card to open the front door. Not that he'd ever broken into anywhere, but it worked in the movies so there must be some basis in reality, right?

The porch creaked and Sam halted, not sure why he bothered. No one lurked in the shadows, but the amusement park felt eerie at night. All of the rides loomed large, hulking dark shadows hovering on deserted fairgrounds.

He'd parked behind the carousel, hoping that anyone who might drive past wouldn't see his vehicle.

The gates had been wide-open. Maybe they didn't ever close. Maybe they were rusted and no longer worked.

Sam touched the doorknob, turning it out of curiosity.

The door opened, with the house left unlocked so anyone could wander in.

He shook his head. Small towns. Alarmed and locked-down, his house in New York could never be broken into except by the most determined and expert of thieves.

He stepped inside and closed the door behind him to block out the wind. He wandered the first floor, not really knowing what he was looking for.

It would have been better to have come in the daytime, but he doubted those women would give an inch now that Violet was pregnant and it was his fault.

Correction, *their* fault.

Violet was an adult, too. It had been consensual sex. So why did Sam feel guilty about going back to New York where he belonged? Why did Chelsea's response still hurt?

He turned all thoughts of that aside. He had this rare, if illegal, opportunity to see the inside of his Gramps's house.

Wanting to take in as much as he could, he swung the flashlight around. Ordinary furniture sat in ordinary configurations.

An old armchair nestled into a corner of the living room looked like it had been shaped by his grandfather's backside over a number of years, maybe a couple of decades.

Sam sat in it, just to sense his Gramps close in this house, to experience a part of his heritage.

If he'd ever taken a few weeks out of his busy life, he could have sat here with Gramps while he still lived in the house. Maybe had breakfasts with him. Gone for walks around the fairgrounds while Gramps showed off everything he'd built with Sam's great-grandfather.

In the beam of his flashlight, it all looked so ordinary, the coffee table and TV and worn sofa, and yet it meant the world to Sam to be here, even too late.

With Gramps's mind definitely going, soon there wouldn't be much left. Then what would remain of him except Sam's memories? Apparently, Sam no longer had even this house or Gramps's stuff.

Or did he?

Was the lease for only the summer? For one year?

For always? Sam didn't know because Gramps couldn't tell him.

Was there an office in the house? There must be someplace where Gramps had done all of his business over the years. Maybe he'd rented an office in town. If so, were there records in the attic?

He walked toward the back of the house, not bothering to hide his actions. Why? The house was empty.

But just past the kitchen, light leaked out from under a door.

Sam paused and held his breath.

The door flew open inward, and a female voice called out, "Honey, is that you? It's about time you got here. I've been here for an hour."

Oh, shit.

Violet. Of all people.

"Honey?" Her voice not as strong now, she sounded hesitant.

Sam had to show himself, if only to stop scaring her.

He stepped into the doorway, the light in the room bright after the dark house. He squinted and lifted his hand to cover his eyes.

"You! What are you doing here?"

The second his eyes adjusted, he recognized fear in hers, and in the arm raised to protect herself.

"God, Violet, stop," he said, pained that she would think he would harm her. "I'm not here to hurt you."

"No? You find out today that I'm pregnant and you think it ruins all of your future plans. Who could blame you if you wanted to get rid of the problem?"

Disbelief surged through him. "Seriously, Violet? You could think that of me?"

She faltered. "What else should I think? You just broke into this house while I'm here alone."

"I didn't know you were here," he explained. "And I didn't break in. The front door was unlocked."

She startled. "It was?"

"Didn't you come in and leave it open?"

"I parked in the backyard. I always come through the back door because the office is right here. I don't know who left the front door unlocked." Her face hardened. "I would have made sure it was locked if I'd known you'd come snooping around."

Anger sizzled in Sam's veins. Sure, he wasn't supposed to be in this house, but he'd never given any indication that he was prone to violence. "I'm not here to steal anything or to murder anyone."

"How would I know that? You're a virtual stranger."

"Who you introduced to your friends as a tenant. Remember? Obviously, you trusted me on some level."

She shrugged. So stubborn. She didn't like to lose.

"You made love with me by the stream. Don't tell me you do that with every stranger who comes through town."

"No. I don't." A huge concession, and one that sounded hard to admit.

"So you have some intuition that I'm not dangerous." He stepped a little farther into the room and said as convincingly as he'd ever claimed anything, "I'm not a violent man."

She must have trusted the sincerity in his voice, somewhat. She retreated behind the desk but stayed coiled to attack. Or so it seemed to Sam. It pained him that she trusted him so little. But then, he hadn't given her a lot to go on, had he?

"I'm serious. I would never hurt you. Okay?" In fact, he'd missed her with an ache that took him by surprise.

When she'd entered the stable today after two weeks of

seeing her only at a distance, it was like a ray of sunshine had entered his life again.

Then she'd dropped her bombshell.

She nodded, face pale in the warm lamplight flooding the room.

God. He'd really frightened her.

"I'm asking only one more time," she said, tone still hard. "I want an answer or I'm calling Cole Payette."

The sheriff. Not good.

"What are you doing in this house?"

Sam heaved a sigh. All he seemed to do these days was screw up. "Apparently, making a big mistake."

She didn't relax.

He could try to bullshit his way out of this, but the time had come for honesty. Not one speck of his subterfuge had gotten him a single answer in the three weeks he'd been in town. Add to that the four days he'd taken to drive across six states with his daughter.

So much time invested for no return. As a businessperson, he knew when to cut his losses.

But he hadn't come here as an astute businessman, rather as a grandson, and all of his decisions had been emotional, no matter how much he'd tried to convince himself otherwise. Chelsea had been right. He should have come here honestly.

Exhausted by pointless dishonesty, he pointed to an armchair in the corner. "Mind if I sit?"

As regal as any queen, Violet gave her consent with a stiff nod and he fell into the chair.

He leaned forward on his elbows and sank his head into his hands. He breathed into his palms, preparing himself for the firestorm that would erupt the second he told Violet who he was.

"My name isn't really Sam Michaels."

She made a scoffing sound. "Surprise, surprise."

"It's Carson Samuel Carmichael."

She stared at him for protracted moments with her mouth open. "You're—"

"Carson's grandson."

Her hands dropped to the desk and she leaned forward, both aggressive and mystified. "But...why hide it?"

"I..." *Oh, crap, how to explain?* "Gramps hasn't been able to tell me what kind of deal he worked out with the rejuvenation committee."

"So you came here to spy on us. Right? You don't trust us."

She was quick. He liked that about her, but maybe not so much at the moment.

"Yes, I came here to spy on you." Before she could gather a lungful of outrage to blast him, he forestalled her. "Understand that I love my grandfather and I thought you were all cheating him. It was my duty to find out as much as I could to protect his interests. To protect *him*."

"To protect your own interests, you mean, don't you? These fairgrounds would be worth a pretty penny if you sold."

He took off the cowboy hat he'd come to kind of like wearing and tossed it onto the desk.

"*No.* I could buy this land a number of times over."

When Violet crossed her arms, cocked one hip and stared, he said, "It's true. I have money. I'm worried about Gramps's money for *his* sake. He put his lifetime into this place. I didn't want to see him robbed." When she didn't look convinced, he went on, "I really, truly came here to protect Gramps from what I thought were a bunch of dishonest women."

"Why would you assume we're dishonest?"

"First, because I didn't know you. I would have trusted in Gramps in his opinion, but he isn't himself anymore."

He had to stop speaking to draw a deep breath. Talking about his grandfather's dementia left him emotional.

"I know," Violet said, her voice saturated with compassion and understanding. He liked her softer side as much as her spirit.

"He told me disturbing things," Sam said, "but then couldn't remember other details I needed to make an informed decision about what was going on here."

She waited.

"The only reasonable conclusion I could come to was to get out here to see what was going on for myself."

"And now that you're here, what do you think?"

In a rush of frustration, he leaned forward. "Nothing. I haven't learned a damned thing! You're the last person I should expect sympathy from, but do you have any idea how rotten it feels that I still don't know if my grandfather is being ripped off?"

"Even after meeting us, you still think we're dishonest?"

Compelled to reveal all that he'd been thinking lately, Sam said, "No. I don't. I like all of you. Tonight, this—" he waved his hand to indicate the house "—was desperation. I wanted to see the house one time before heading back home."

She flinched at the reminder that he wouldn't be staying.

"Why couldn't you have asked?"

"Because it would have blown my cover."

"But why have a cover? Why not come to town and just ask us what was going on? We would have shown you the contract Carson signed."

Sam sat up. "He signed a *contract*? But…he told me he hadn't."

"Of course we have a contract. Cripes, how stupid do you think we are to come into this venture without making everything legal?" She stretched to open a drawer but then shot him a look. "Don't answer that. It's obvious how stupid you thought we were."

"Not stupid. Dishonest."

"Just as bad. Here." She tossed him a sheaf of stapled papers. "Read 'em and weep."

Sam caught the contract and leaned toward one of the lamps. He did, indeed, read it. The entire thing. Every word.

Dear God, Gramps had gotten it all so wrong.

They'd leased the land from him for one year for a thousand dollars. If they made a profit, Carson would receive a healthy percentage with the understanding that the rest would go toward improving the town, after expenses.

"Carson told me none of this," he said faintly. "Not one word. He said you gave him one dollar for the lease. He doesn't even have a memory of there being a contract."

"If you knew his mind was going, why didn't you take that into account before rushing out here to pretend to be something, someone, you weren't?"

"Because I didn't know Gramps's mind was going. I had no idea. I call him every week. I thought he was good until I came here and saw some of his odd behavior. I began to doubt everything he was telling me."

"But not enough to come out of hiding."

"No, not enough to stop spying."

Sam checked out Gramps's office. From this room, he'd conducted business for six decades or more.

"Why was the house included in the lease?"

"*For this office and Carson's records.* The six of us? We've never done anything like this before. We're ignorant about pulling off an event this large. It's intimidating."

She walked to a bookcase lined with binder after binder. "Here, in all of these binders, is the history of the fair and all of the information that Carson wrote up over the years. A lot of it is outdated, but not all. It's like a really great instruction manual."

Sam was silent for a moment, then he asked, "Where do we go from here?"

"We? There is no *we*. You're returning to New York City. Remember?" Still and contained, she sat down quietly. "Could our lives be any different?"

He shook his head. "No."

"Even if you were willing to live here in Rodeo—" she raised a hand when he would have objected "—I know that's an impossibility. You aren't cut out for life here."

He wanted to argue with her. He could live here, happily, but the business, his friends and his homes beckoned, as did his revenge. Okay, skip the rest. It was all about revenge.

Somehow, someway, he would make Tiffany and her father regret the day they'd betrayed him.

"Besides," Violet continued, "after the way you've lied, I could never trust you again."

"This has been an aberration. I'm a trustworthy guy. Honest."

"I can't trust, Sam. Ever. I have my reasons." Violet sighed. "Let's go to the kitchen. This story's going to take a while. I need coffee."

He followed her and sat on a kitchen stool at a worn counter while she made a pot of coffee.

Sam declined, but she doctored one for herself. He waited. Whatever she had to share looked heavy.

VIOLET COULDN'T SIT STILL, not when she had to tell her story twice in one day. Not when the story pained her.

She did, though. Tell it, that was, and Sam listened and reacted with as much compassion as her friends had, to her surprise.

"Violet, I'm so sorry. It shouldn't have happened." He scrubbed his shadowed jawline. "I don't understand why your mother didn't support you."

"It was fear. I think she was afraid she would never find another man to support her emotionally."

"Have you ever tried to contact her?"

"Only when my aunt died but Mom didn't respond. She wasn't Aunt Belinda's sister. I guess once Mom pawned me off on Dad's sister, she thought her connection to that side of the family ended. She didn't respond, nor did she attend the funeral."

That had hurt but had confirmed for Vy that she no longer had a mother.

"So I haven't contacted her for years, no. Except today I thought about it. Soon she'll have another grandchild."

Vy felt herself tear up. God, all of this emotion disgusted her.

She shook her head. "But why would it matter? She didn't accept her first grandchild. She urged me to put her up for adoption without a single qualm. Then she got rid of me."

"But that baby was also her boyfriend's, which would have been painful for her no matter how it came about. This one isn't."

"Sam, I'm not going to reach out. That relationship is dead. It's been fourteen years. She knows where I am. There hasn't been a single letter or Christmas card or phone call. Her silence speaks volumes."

He grimaced. "I guess it does."

She leaned on the counter, elbows locked, and hung her head. Life was never easy or straightforward.

"I'm so tired, Sam. I just want life to stop for a few minutes."

"Then maybe it should."

"What do you mean?"

"Come here," Sam said, holding out his hand across the counter.

"Why?"

"My God, you are prickly."

She smiled. "Always."

"It's a good thing I like you that way, but what you need right now is some Sam Carmichael comfort."

"It's going to be hard to think of you as Carmichael instead of Michaels."

"You're smart. You'll manage."

He took her hand, drew her around the counter and led her to the living room.

"Earlier, I noticed a fireplace in here." Sam knelt in front of the hearth. "Do you know if this thing works?"

"Yes. The house is drafty in the wintertime. We used the fireplace all winter."

"Good. Grab a couple of those afghans and lay them out in front of the hearth."

"We are *not* making love."

"Okay."

"I mean it."

Sam turned to look at her. "I said okay, Violet."

But she *wanted* to make love.

He must have seen her desire in her eyes, because he asked, "Are you sure that we shouldn't just hold each other?"

"No," she admitted. "I'm not sure of anything."

"Me, either." He smiled. "You look as in need of a hug tonight as I feel. I just found out I've made an utter fool of myself in front of an entire town. My grandfather is disappearing and now, too late, I find I've missed too much of his life."

Vy heard the depth of regret in him, in the way his voice cracked.

Sam blew on the paper and kindling bits he'd already lit with a match from a tube on top of the mantel. "*Do* you need to be held tonight? *I* do."

She did need to be held, especially by Sam. She was angry with him and betrayed and hurt but she *liked* him. She liked his soft side, his caring and nurturing side. She liked the way he moved, with efficiency and purpose even while his silly grin threatened to appear. She liked how easygoing he was…when they weren't fighting. She liked how he could take charge, like right now when she was vulnerable but didn't want to admit it.

What if they had the same goals, the same purpose in life? What would it be like to live with a Sam who was laidback, funny and sweet all of the time?

Temptation.

No. It wouldn't happen.

She had told Sam everything. He hadn't judged her. But all of this brought back to Vy how much she'd screwed up when young, and of how little she deserved to be happy when her mother was so badly hurt. Her mother had seen every action of Vy's as betrayal, even though it had protected her from losing her life savings.

Except only Vy believed that. Her mother never had.

She didn't deserve a life with Sam. She didn't deserve *all the time* with Sam. She didn't deserve *more*.

"Stop that," Sam said, a new fire blazing behind him.

"Stop what?"

"Whatever heavy thinking you're doing that's putting that look on your face. Tonight it's just you, me and now. Nothing else. Let's hold each other."

"Okay."

She would not say no to tonight, not on her life. She wanted his arms around her with a hunger that shocked her.

He would leave soon and she would be alone to raise their child. She should scorn him on principle but she needed more of the *more* she'd experienced with him.

Living on principle made for lonely nights. She'd done that for too long.

Sam might be the man who angered her more than any ever had, except for Ray, but she wanted his arms around her.

If that made her weak, well, then, so be it.

She lay down and cuddled against him with a long sigh.

The strength of his hold, the heat of his body, the depth of her need had her reaching for more of that *more*.

He sighed, too, and responded.

They made love softly, gently, for a long time.

At one point, they heard the front door open and then Honey's voice called out, "Violet? Is that you?"

"Yes. Don't come in."

"Why not?"

"She knows I come here late to work and to think," Vy whispered, so Sam would understand the revolving front door after midnight. "Sometimes she shows up when she can't sleep."

"Honey, go away," she said out loud.

"Was that Sam's truck parked behind the carousel?"

Sam swore under his breath. "Yes, Honey. That's my vehicle."

"Vy...do you want him here?"

"Yes, I do, Honey. I really do."

"Okay. I'll leave you two alone."

Vy heard the front door close and the lock click into place, as Honey made sure no one else interrupted them.

It didn't much matter who had forgotten to lock it earlier. Sam was with her now for one night.

One precious night.

The sex, the holding, the comforting and the murmured words lasted until dawn. Vy reveled in it.

"Violet?" Sam sounded as replete as Vy felt.

"Yes?"

"You did the right thing all of those years ago, even if your mother didn't believe it. Even if she never does."

"Maybe."

He shook her shoulder. "Yes," he insisted. "Imagine if you hadn't. Imagine the state your mother would have been in if Ray had taken all of her money and fled town."

"I guess I was so overwhelmed by the reality of everything that happened that I lost sight of that. I don't know what Mom would have done or how she would have survived."

"Remember that, Violet. You are an amazing person. What you did for your mother at such a young age took courage. Afterward you were violated and then abandoned. You are a rock. You are the best person I've ever met."

Vy struggled not to cry. She preferred to be strong. Not that she would ever see tears in others as weakness, but she found them so in herself.

"It's time," Sam whispered. "I'm sorry."

Vy understood that his apology covered everything, the way he'd come to town, their carelessness in conceiving a baby and his inability to stay.

They stood and dressed. When fully clothed, she turned to Sam. He kissed her one last time, turned and left the house. Vy stared at the closed front door for a long time, then got into her own car around the back.

At home, she trudged upstairs knowing she'd seen Sam for the last time as a lover, and maybe as a friend. From now on, she expected their correspondence to be through lawyers and banks. No love letters. No romance.

But Sam had given her two gifts. First, the baby in her belly. Until now she hadn't realized how much she'd missed the little girl she'd given up for adoption. How much that had left a gaping hole in her.

This baby was a gift.

Second, he'd laid her mind to rest about her mother. Yes, Mom had been devastated by Vy's apparent betrayal, but she would have been lost without money and a means of support.

Maybe Mom was living a lonely life or maybe she'd found a more honest partner than Ray. Vy didn't know.

What she did know was that telling her friends and Sam about it, and receiving their support, had given her the first peace she'd felt in years.

Now, to get on with the rest of her life.

Chapter Twelve

Sam returned to Travis's house, showered, put on his work clothes and walked out to the stable, where he found comfort in the daily routine.

Last night had been… Well, he couldn't think about it or he would become overwhelmed with sadness.

He heard Travis in the office at the back. Sam went to him.

"Can I talk to you?" Sam asked.

Travis looked up from the book he'd been studying. "Sure. What is it?"

"On second thought, I'd like to include Rachel in this conversation."

Travis frowned but nodded. "At breakfast, then?"

"Good." Sam returned to his chores. He hadn't been paid a cent in his time here outside room and board, but the work had been more satisfying than most anything he'd ever done. Simple and honest.

Not that he would ever consider becoming either a cowboy or a rancher. He knew his own character.

At breakfast, with the family seated around the kitchen table, including Chelsea, Sam said, "My name isn't Sam Michaels. It's Carson Samuel Carmichael."

A breath whooshed out of Rachel. Chelsea stared at him.

"Thanks," she said.

He glanced at her. "For what?"

"For finally doing the right thing. For telling the truth."

He smiled, but it felt grim. A day late and a dollar short. Yes, he should have been honest from the start but Gramps meant the world to him. How could Sam have known Gramps got it all wrong and not the women?

"You're Carson's grandson?" Rachel asked.

"Yes."

"But why didn't you tell us?"

"I came here to spy on the revival committee." He explained to Travis and Rachel everything that he'd told Violet last night. "I was motivated by love and worry for my grandfather. I protect my family fiercely."

Travis nodded. He would understand the sentiment, if not the methods used.

"If I'd known all of you women beforehand, I wouldn't have reacted the way I did. I thought you were trying to rip him off."

Rachel digested all of that and then stared at him, shocked. "Oh, no."

"What?" Sam asked.

"I said some nasty things about Carson's grandson in front of you."

"Yes, you did." Sam grinned. "And thought even worse than you said, I'll bet."

"Yes. I did. But you're a nice man."

"I am. I'm worried about Gramps and his deteriorating state of mind."

Rachel frowned. "We all are. He's so dear to us. He's been part of our lives forever. I hate to see his mind drift away."

"I'm going to come back and visit him lots," Chelsea said defiantly.

"Anytime you want to visit Rodeo, you come and stay with us, okay?"

"I would like that, Rachel." Chelsea shot a rebellious glance at Sam.

"That's fine with me, Chelsea," he said quietly.

Her tight shoulders eased a bit. At some point, she would learn that he had her best interests at heart. Since the day he'd lambasted both Gramps and Chelsea for treating him badly, she'd been better. Not perfect, but better. In time, he hoped, the destruction caused by her parents' divorce would have less and less of an impact.

That afternoon, they visited Gramps and told him.

"So you're really leaving?" His eyes watered.

"We'll be back," Sam assured him, but he couldn't say when, knowing how much work starting a business entailed. He'd already had to do a certain amount of it long-distance. He shouldn't even have been in Rodeo at such a crucial time.

But Gramps…well, he was worth it.

Sam regretted deeply that he had distrusted those great women. If only he'd suspected Gramps's state of mind before he left home.

They hugged Gramps for long, long moments, no one wanting to let go, to make this goodbye real.

The next two days passed in a blur for Sam. He'd never had such a crisis of conscience. He knew he had to leave. He didn't want to. He had to. His head ached.

He visited the local legal office and had them draw up documents giving Sam power of attorney over Gramps's affairs. With his doctor as witness that Gramps was still able to make the decision to sign the papers, and was cognizant of doing so, Sam had everything finalized.

He breathed a sigh. Relief. Thank goodness Gramps

was cared for. Sam could rest more easily knowing that he could take care of Gramps even from a distance.

Next, he visited Michael Moreno's ranch where he met Samantha Read, a strikingly beautiful, happy, levelheaded woman. Where money matters for the fair were concerned, she would be dealing with him from now on, not Gramps.

He met Michael, a taciturn, salt-of-the-earth kind of man, steady of character with a good firm handshake. He met their four children. A combined family. Cute little kids and one quiet older boy. More power to them if they could make it work.

He returned to the ranch and helped Travis out with as many chores as he could to ease his burden. Sam had become pretty good at a lot of it.

He packed his bags.

On the day of departure, he loaded the SUV.

It took them ages to leave because Tori wouldn't let go of Chelsea. Or was it the other way around? Sam couldn't tell. All he knew was that two young girls stood in front of him with their hearts breaking.

They'd only been here three and a half weeks. How could the girls have grown so close in so short a time?

Why not, Sam? You fell in love with Violet that quickly. Love! Whoa. No. No way.

Sam leaned against the vehicle with his heart pounding out of his chest, thinking about the night they'd spent together in Gramps's house. The tenderness and passion and deep connection had cemented themselves in his heart, a piece of him now, part of his life no matter how far away from Rodeo and Violet that he drove.

His experience here had changed him.

Violet had changed him.

With her big, bold personality and generous heart, she'd given him more than he'd ever expected to find in this small town. Even after learning of his betrayal, she'd laid herself bare and had made herself vulnerable to him. So much courage.

He would treasure memories of that night forever.

His phone rang, cutting through his thoughts and the girls' sobbing goodbyes.

He answered. Tom Hudson, the lawyer for his new company, with questions. When did he expect to arrive in the city? When could they talk? They needed to book one final appointment.

Barely able to concentrate, Sam named a time. He couldn't bring his partners' faces to mind, let alone details of the business.

He'd been away too long and had gone too far both in distance and emotionally.

It would come back to him. He straightened away from the vehicle. He would get his business mojo back. No problem.

"Chelsea," he said. "We have to go."

He shook Travis's hand. "You turned out to be a pretty good ranch hand," the man said.

If Sam had stayed, he knew he could have forged a friendship with Travis.

He turned to Rachel with his arms slightly open. Would she let him hug her?

She did, and he smiled from ear to ear. He liked her and hugged her hard. She was smart and talented and a good friend to Violet.

Their leaving more difficult than Sam could have possibly anticipated, he turned away to discreetly wipe a tear.

A grown man like him crying. He needed to stop, but it was hard with the girls' faucets running nonstop. How was he going to get Chelsea away from here?

Again he said to her, "We have to go."

She trudged to the car and got in.

He drove away without looking back, but Chelsea stared through the back window, waving, until the old Victorian and its inhabitants couldn't be any larger than dots in the distance.

She turned around. "Can we stop at the fairground?"

"Yes." He had planned to anyway, to say goodbye to a place that mattered to him, that was no longer a dream created by his grandfather's stories but a reality seen with his own eyes.

So what if it still needed work? There was magic in the place. The impulse that had started the women on their revival of it had been sound. They were smart. They would do well.

If he wished that he could be here to see it happen, he squashed that sentiment ruthlessly.

"I'm coming back in August." Chelsea sounded less defiant and more confident.

He smiled at her. "That's a good idea."

"Will you come with me?"

"I'll try." He sensed her withdrawal, knowing that in parent speak "I'll try" most often meant *no*.

Could he bring himself to come back then and see Violet swollen with their child?

He swore and slammed his hand on the steering wheel.

"Dad?"

"Sorry. I didn't realize leaving would be this hard. It sucks."

"It really does." He heard no criticism in her voice. Maybe his declaration that this was hard for him, too, made her realize that he wasn't leaving this town unscathed. He cared. God, did he care.

He pulled onto the shoulder and got out.

Sam approached the fence, drinking in every detail of the half-revived fair.

The magical carousel ride gleamed in the sun. He should be here to take a ride when it was running, especially with his daughter. It would be amazing.

Would the ladies bring Gramps here so he could see it? Probably. They liked him. They respected him. Now that Sam knew them, he understood they would do right by Carson Carmichael.

FROM THE CORNER of her eye, Violet noticed Rachel enter the diner with her two girls.

Tori's eyes were red, her little face puffy.

So, Sam and Chelsea had left.

Why hadn't Violet felt it, like having the breath sucked out of her? But no. Outside, it was a normal sunny day. Inside the diner, customers placed orders and expected service.

She approached Rachel's table. "They're gone, aren't they?"

Tori started to cry. Violet sat in the booth and gathered the child into her arms. "You'll be okay, sweetheart. It will take a while but we'll all be okay."

If only she could believe that in her heart. Sure, she would do all of the right things. She would put one foot in front of the other day after day, but a piece of her was now missing and she wanted it back. That wasn't going to happen.

A heart, once given, could not be taken back.

"You love him," Rachel said. "For the first time since I've known you, your face is an open book. You love that guy already. If you didn't, you wouldn't have given him so much of your attention and time and emotion, even anger, since the first moment he arrived in town."

"I don't know why I love him."

"I do. He's a decent man. Even though he came here dishonestly, his motivations were good. He wanted to protect Carson. He loves him even more than we do. I can't fault him for that."

"That doesn't mean that he loves me."

"When you enter a room, he lights up. His eyes never leave you."

"That only means he's attracted to me physically."

"I've had that man in my house for the past three weeks. He's deeper than that. He cares."

"But not enough to stay."

"No. Not enough to stay."

SAM LEANED HIS arms on the top of the fence. Chelsea joined him, crying as though her heart was shattering.

Maybe it was.

His heart sure felt that way.

"Chelsea, I don't understand. You were raised in New York. You're urban through and through. You have a bunch of friends."

"Yes." She nodded and hiccupped. "So?"

"So why do you like it here so much that you want to live here? I assume you're crying so hard because you'd like to stay here indefinitely."

"It's special, Dad. There are really nice people. There's no noise. There are animals *everywhere*."

"You don't think maybe it's just the novelty of being in some place different?"

"No, Dad."

"You don't think it might wear off?"

"No. I really like it here."

Was it truly that simple for her? Could she make the change so easily?

After a while, Sam noticed a man watching them. He stood beside an old ride with a toolbox in his hand.

Sam glanced at him, did a double take, then stared.

"Chelsea?"

"Yeah?"

"Dry your eyes for me, possum, and check out that guy standing beside the carousel. What do you think of him?"

"What do you mean? He's just a guy." She pulled a tissue out of her pocket, dried her tears and looked again. "Oh! Dad, doesn't he sort of look like you? A lot? Like not exactly, but it's like you could be brothers except that his hair is dark."

"I was thinking the same thing. He looks hostile, though. Wonder why?"

The man approached and asked, "You're a Carmichael, aren't you?" Actually, it was more a statement than a question, and his tone was definitely hostile.

Sam nodded. "Who are you?"

The guy didn't respond. He looked maybe five years older than Sam.

Sam had an eerie feeling that some things were starting to fall into place. "What's your mother's first name?" Sam asked, remembering the story of his dad leaving town because of a woman.

"Candace."

Sam's eyes widened. That had been her name.

"So he mentioned my mom, did he?"

"By *he*, I assume you mean Carson II?"

The man's belligerent chin jutted forward. "That's right."

Sam smiled but grimly. "No, I'm afraid he didn't. Sorry."

"Figures." He stalked away.

Sam had a half brother he'd never known. This, *he*, was

what Sam's father had left behind. He was a responsibility Sam's father had run from.

So what had happened? Dad had gotten Candace pregnant but had refused to give up his dreams of an Ivy League education out east? Had Dad run from her rather than take responsibility? Or had he not believed the child was his?

Sam could tell him that he was, beyond a shadow of a doubt.

Had Dad been nothing so much as a coward? Sam had never thought so, but he'd left a child behind without a second thought. Had he at least sent financial support? Sam didn't think so. That guy had been bitter and angry and ready to spit on anyone with the last name Carmichael.

How had Gramps not known he had a grandson here in town? How did the whole town not know of it? Had Candace left town and come home later with a child and maybe a new husband? Someone had said she had been married.

All of these years of being an only child, Sam could have had a brother. He could have known his half sibling.

He would have liked that.

He glanced at Chelsea quietly sniffling beside him. Sam was about to do the same thing to her. How like his father was he?

All of his life, Sam had striven to please his parents because he thought kids were supposed to. Dad had been cutthroat in business—the acquisition of more and more money important to him.

Sam realized now, looking back, how much he'd been like his dad at times, and how his parents had nudged him toward Tiffany.

Look how it had all turned out. He'd done everything his parents had asked of him, and all he had left to show for it outside a healthy bank account was a need for revenge that was maybe ruining his character.

His phone rang. He checked the number. John Raven. Tired of his new business partners checking in, Sam took the call, but nothing John said made sense. He might as well have been speaking gibberish. Sam's ears rang. His head ached.

He asked John to repeat himself, but Sam still couldn't process it. He realized why.

The business didn't matter to him. It no longer meant a thing. None of it mattered because revenge was a hollow aspiration.

Success is the best revenge.

Yes, but did it have to be measured only financially? Couldn't success be measured by the amount of love in your life? By the quality of your friends? By the outstanding beauty and generosity of your lover?

He hung up on John. He couldn't stand another second of useless chatter. He turned off his phone so the man wouldn't call back.

What he really wanted to do was chuck the thing as far across the fields as he could and never have any contact with his partners, his business and his lawyers again.

He wanted peace. And happiness. And Violet.

Chelsea leaned her head on his shoulder. She must be really upset to seek comfort from him even when she was so angry with him.

He wrapped his arm around her and pulled her around to stand in front of him. She watched him with a puzzled frown.

Cupping her face in the palms of his hands, he kissed her forehead, leaving his mouth to rest there for a moment, inhaling the essence of his daughter. He would know her anywhere.

He pulled back and stared into her eyes. "You have been the best thing that ever happened in my life. The absolute best. Better than any business success. Better than any money. Better than *anything*."

Chelsea's eyes filled with tears.

"I love you with all of my heart and soul."

"I love you, too, Daddy, but I don't want to leave here."

"Neither do I. Should we go back and I'll get married to Violet and get to know our baby and make more babies?"

"Do you mean it?" She looked afraid to hope.

"From the deepest corner of my heart."

"Yeah!" She ran for the car. "Hurry, Dad! Hurry before Violet starts to hate you so badly for leaving that she'll never love you again."

Sam started the vehicle and pulled away from the shoulder. "You do understand that you'll have to work your butt off this summer?"

"At the fair?" She looked hopeful.

"Nothing that much fun. I'll hire a tutor and you'll have lessons every day. You'll do homework and you'll write essays and tests and do whatever else you have to do so you can enter the correct grade here in town in September."

"Okay." She sounded docile and he liked it, a good change from 'tude girl.

"I shouldn't have taken you out of school and dragged you across the country."

"Yes, you should have, Dad. I know I was in a bad mood, but it's the best trip I've ever taken."

"Really?"

"I'm so angry about Mom's behavior and on some level I think I blamed you, too. Maybe if you'd kept her happy she wouldn't have gone to another man."

He'd wondered that himself.

"But that's not true. Mom made her own decisions. If

she'd wanted more happiness in her marriage, she should have worked harder. I think a lot of the time Mom coasted."

"I think so, too."

"You're never getting back together and it's time for me to accept that."

"Great growing-up wisdom, possum. I've had growing to do, too, and there's still more to be done. At some point, I'll have to forge a relationship with that guy who's my half brother. I'm determined to fix my father's mistakes."

He grinned at his daughter. "I have a brother and you have an uncle. Woo-hoo."

Sam's foot hit the gas pedal. "Let's go propose to Violet."

They broke the speed limit on the way back to town.

Ears ringing, Sam rehearsed what he would say to Violet. How could he win her when he'd already said goodbye?

On Main Street, he thought he heard a siren but kept driving.

Pulling into a parking spot in front of the diner with a squeal of tires, he jumped out of the vehicle and raced to the front door.

"Hey," someone yelled. "Stop right there."

Sam ran into the Summertime Diner. Everyone stopped eating and turned to stare. No one spoke.

Where was Violet?

"Where is she?" he asked, frantic. Now that he'd made the decision to live here and to be with Violet forever, he needed it to happen *now*.

Someone pointed to the kitchen.

"Violet," he called. "Get out here this minute."

She came out, one haughty eyebrow raised as though to say "Nobody bosses me around."

God, he loved her. He loved every single thing about her.

Someone grabbed his arm and tried to whip him around,

a man in uniform, but Sam could take his eyes from Violet for only a moment. Now that he was here, all of the lovely things he'd rehearsed in the car fled his brain.

"You just sped into town like a maniac. License and registration, now," the man said.

Sam pulled out his wallet and handed it to the man.

The cop wouldn't take it. "Sir! Remove your license."

Instead, Sam took out a wad of bills and held them out. He thought it might be about five hundred bucks.

"Are you trying to bribe an officer of the law?"

"That's for the speeding ticket," he murmured while he watched Violet walk toward him, every nuance of her beautiful body dear and familiar to him.

"You can't—"

"Cole, be quiet." It sounded like Honey's voice. "I want to hear what Sam has to say."

Sam dropped the money and his wallet, took Violet's hands and urged her closer.

Wrapping his arms around her, he untied her apron and gently lifted it over her head.

"Will!" he yelled

"Yeah?" The voice was surprisingly close.

Sam glanced over. Will stood on the other side of the counter. Sam tossed Violet's apron to the man.

"Take over for a while. Violet's taking a break. Make my daughter a banana split. And anything else she wants."

Will grinned so widely dimples showed in his usually stoic face. A female nearby sighed. Will frowned.

"Violet, come upstairs with me."

Before she could answer, Chelsea said, "No, Dad, you have to stay down here."

Sam laughed. He kissed the backs of Violet's hands.

"Some things are meant to be private."

"Daaad. You can do all of that smooching later. First

you have to ask her. You have to do it here. I want to hear all of it."

Sam spoke from his heart. "Violet, I've been a fool. I came here all wrong. I should have been honest from the start. Here is my honesty now. From the first second I laid eyes on you, I knew you were special. I love you. I want to marry you. I want to start our family *together*. I want to do it here in Rodeo. I want to stay."

"That was great, Dad, but you have to actually *ask* her."

"Chelsea, I can do this without your help." He smiled. "Violet, will you marry me?"

"Yes." Then Violet Summer burst into tears.

"Stop. Don't cry. What's wrong?"

"I'm happy. I'm really, really happy."

"Me, too!" Chelsea said and a roomful of people burst into laughter.

Sam looked around. Apparently, word had spread like wildfire, or else him screeching through town had brought people out.

As well as the people seated in booths, there were others crowded in the doorway, including Honey and Nadine with huge smiles on their faces.

Petite, gorgeous, misty-eyed Honey Armstrong grasped one of the sheriff's arms in hers. Tall, handsome Cole Payette stared down at her, wonderment in his expression.

"Okay," Chelsea announced. "Now you can go upstairs and get up close and personal."

"Chelsea!" Sam protested. "You're only thirteen."

"Going on forty," Violet said, her voice still sounding damp.

"I'll stay down here to celebrate with a banana split. Or two." Chelsea giggled and threw herself into Sam's arms. "I'm so happy. I love you, Dad."

Taking the small souvenir purse out of his pocket, now

thick with quarters, he gave it to his daughter. "Knock yourself out, possum."

She grinned and sat at the counter.

Life was perfect, better than perfect. It was sublime. Sam's success included a child he adored, a woman he loved and an unborn child to get to know.

He planned to be there every step of the way, through every doctor's visit and every breathing exercise. He'd missed these things the first time around with Chelsea because of building a new company.

He didn't have that to worry about now. There would be something for him to do in his future. He hated to be idle, but an answer, an opportunity, would show itself in time.

Rodeo needed more than just a rodeo every summer to keep it going. It needed industry. Sam knew a lot of people, men and women with influence and money. He could do something for this town.

At the moment, though, all of his creative focus was locked on Violet and celebration.

He took her hand and got out while the getting was good, the townspeople stepping aside and making a path for them to go celebrate their love.

Once outside on the sidewalk and heading to the apartment door, Sam noted Maxine rushing toward the diner.

"Is it true?" She ignored Sam and asked Violet, "Are you getting married?"

There was no happiness in her tone, only belligerence and a vague disappointment directed toward Violet.

What had happened in her past? A bad marriage? A betraying spouse?

Sam understood, but with the blazing light of the newly converted, he also knew that bitterness and single-minded revenge could rob a person of the joys of love.

"Max…" Violet started, but Sam interrupted, intuiting

that Max had powerful negativity going on that had nothing to do with either of them.

He sensed how to distract her so she wouldn't ruin this moment.

"I need to talk to you."

Max ignored him.

"About the rodeo."

She glanced his way.

"And how to make it different and unique."

He had her full attention.

"Polo."

"What?"

"A polo match."

She started to turn away but halted when Sam continued, "I have friends with more money than they know what to do with. They would donate horses, stable staff, time and money to an event like this."

"Donate?" she whispered.

"Everything. You could start your rodeo off with an exciting event that wouldn't cost you a cent."

She hesitated.

He leaned close. "Have you ever seen a polo match?"

She shook her head.

"It's fast-paced and gripping. Fans love it. It gets the crowd excited." He sweetened the deal. "You could do something fun like pit my polo-playing friends against local cowboys or rodeo riders. Put the cowboys on polo ponies and watch the sparks fly. East versus West. Urban versus rural. Let's see if they can keep their seats in polo saddles. Everyone loves a competition."

Max's eyes lit up, as though already envisioning the match. She punched Sam's shoulder. "We'll talk."

Sam rubbed his shoulder. The woman was tough.

She stepped away to the diner doorway before spinning back to address Sam with a stern finger pointed toward his chest.

"You hurt Violet and there won't be a spot on this earth where you'll be able to hide from me." She entered the diner.

"Whew! She's intense."

"Don't be hard on her, Sam. Her life has been difficult. She loves hard. She's a mother hen who protects those she loves."

"More like a banty rooster." Sam appraised Violet. "You don't look offended."

"I'm not. I'm happy. I live in a town I love. I have friends who support me without boundaries. I love a great guy. And I'm finally free to be me."

"And who is that?"

"The woman I've pretended to be all along is the woman I have a right to be. I've earned everything I have, including this town's respect. I finally understand how much I deserve in this life."

"You deserve it all, Violet, and more."

They walked upstairs and entered her apartment. "I like this place," Sam said. "It's homey."

"I don't know how I'm going to keep the baby here, though. There's hardly enough room."

"*We* are going to get a house. How does that sound?" Sam turned her toward him. "You're no longer alone, Violet. I understand your need for independence and I honor it, but you don't have to make every decision on your own anymore."

"A house would be wonderful."

"I wonder…" Sam hated to dream but nothing ventured, nothing gained. "I wonder if we could live in Gramps's house on the fairgrounds. Or is that too unconventional?"

"I love it! Sam, look at me. Do I look conventional to you? It would be amazing to raise a child there."

A grin split Sam's face. "It would, wouldn't it?"

Violet took his hand and led him to her bedroom, kissing him before he had a chance to check it out.

"I love you, Violet. Now and for always."

"I love you, too, Sam."

They made love with sunlight streaming across the bed and warming Sam's back.

Afterward, her head resting on Sam's shoulder, Violet murmured, "You do realize the whole town knows what we're doing up here, right? By now every phone call has been answered and every text read. They all know that Violet Summer succumbed to the big-city boy's charms and is going to marry him."

The thought filled Sam with good will and he laughed. "I'll bet it's good for business. Most of the town is downstairs right now, guaranteed. How much do you want to bet Will's swamped?"

Violet shook her head. "Nah. Honey's waitressing. Max is probably pouring coffee. Nadine's cutting up pies and serving them."

"How do you know?"

"They're my friends."

Sam loved the simplicity of that statement and the way it made Violet sound so content. She'd been through a lot, but being a strong woman, she had thrived.

She would thrive even more because Sam planned to shower her with love for the rest of their lives.

Chapter Thirteen

Sam held Violet for too long, afraid to let her go. After finally coming to his senses and realizing how much he loved this woman, he feared the dream would go up in smoke if he opened his eyes. Or let go of her.

"It's okay, Sam. I'm not going anywhere."

"How did you know I was worried?"

"You're holding me pretty tightly." Laughter rang in her voice.

He eased his grip a bit. "I'm not going anywhere, either."

"This is nothing like New York City."

"I know. I think that's why I like it. I like the town. I like the people. I like and love you."

"You're absolutely certain? Because I will never want to live in the big city."

"I'm positive. I'll want to visit my family. I would like to take you to meet them and to show you my favorite spots in New York. It's an amazing city. But I want to live here. Chelsea wants to live here, too. Don't ask me why. She never complained about New York."

"Good."

"Now that that's settled, I want to talk about the revival of the fair."

Sam sensed her pulling away emotionally.

"Why?"

"I have some ideas."

"Why? Don't start taking over. The big-city guy teaching the small-town girls how to run a business properly."

That wasn't what was happening.

"For God's sake, don't start mansplaining things to us. *We* know this country. *We* know what people here like."

"I know. But hear me out. What did you think of the polo match? Could it fly here?"

"Oh! You're asking my opinion."

"Yes. As you said, you know these people. Would it fly?"

"So you were serious. I don't know. Why on earth would anyone here want to watch that?"

"Do you know what I've noticed since I got here?"

"No. What?"

"There's a huge amount of emotion invested in the country-versus-city mentality. How do you think I learned how to ride? By playing amateur polo."

"Sam, I'm still not seeing it."

"Okay, so as I told Max, I persuade all of my polo buddies, who, by the way, have big money, to donate their time, horses and money to the fair. They come out here and bring all of our horses. We have a match against cowboys on their horses."

"Can you actually do that?"

"I have no idea, but it's at least worth looking into."

"I'm not sure cowboys would want to do it."

"I saw a rodeo once. Those guys are insanely competitive. Polo playing is a brutally demanding sport, hard on both players and horses. By the time your cowboys are finished, they'll have a new respect for polo players."

Sam started to get excited. "Then we also have the polo players compete in rodeo events like barrel racing and cattle roping. By the time they're through, they'll have respect for the work that cowboys and ranchers do. What do you think?"

"I think it has a lot of merit. I'll present it to the girls the next time we get together. Or maybe Max already has. They're probably all downstairs discussing it right now."

"Probably. I'll talk to my friends to drum up interest. I'll have takers for sure. These guys might be businessmen, but where polo is concerned, they're tough and competitive. They would consider this a challenge."

"Speaking of challenges, you do understand that you and I are in for a few of them in our life together?"

Sam rested his forehead on Violet's. "I'm up for it. I've never felt as happy or fulfilled as I have with you, even when we were fighting."

Violet laughed. "There will most certainly be fighting over the years."

"We can survive any disagreements as long as we come together in love afterward."

"I think I can handle that."

Sam grinned. "I'm going to enjoy make-up sex with you."

"Let's start now."

"But we haven't argued."

"We don't need to. All of our sex is going to be great sex. I can feel it in my bones."

Sam ran a hand over her softly rounded hip. "I love you, Violet."

"And I love you, Mr. Pretend Cowboy. Let's celebrate our happiness."

An hour later, they showered, dressed and went down to the diner.

They peeked in through the window. The place was packed, with *everyone* there, as though they'd been waiting for the happy couple to show up.

What if they'd decided to stay in bed for the rest of the evening and all night? Would the town have stayed here, too?

Then again, they would know that Sam wouldn't abandon his daughter.

Chelsea sat at the counter. Will stood across from her. They played cards. Were those coins in front of them? Was Will teaching his daughter how to gamble?

Sam stalked toward the door.

When he and Violet stepped into the diner, everyone cheered as though they'd done something stupendous.

Jeez. They'd only been doing what every adult in this room was capable of doing.

Sam's cheeks reddened. He didn't consider himself the blushing type, but this town was making his sex life public, for Pete's sake.

Tori ran over and tugged on Violet's skirt.

She bent forward. "What is it, sweetheart?"

"Chels is going to live here." Tori let out a tiny squeal.

"I know. I'm happy, too. Chelsea is going to become my friend."

"She's already my friend. Now she's gonna be my big sister. We pinkie sweared." She held up her tiny pinkie finger.

Violet kissed her forehead and sent her back to her table.

Violet directed her attention to the room and spoke up. "I'm only going to say this once because I don't want any gossip about it. I don't want to be pestered about it. I don't want any sly glances or speculation. I'm pregnant. Okay? End of story."

After a brief silence, Lester Voile said, "We already know that, Vy. Congratulations." He got out of his booth and approached, pulling a folded sheet of paper out of his pocket.

"I got this recipe I want you to try. I got it off the Food Network. I think I wrote it all down right."

Sam felt Violet shake beneath his arm. He looked down at her. Tears streamed down her cheeks while she laughed. Soon her laughter burst out of her in great, full guffaws.

Sam joined her. So did the rest of the room.

He'd never seen Violet so happy.

Sam's anticipated task? To make that joy last a lifetime.

On Christmas Day, Sam sat on the sofa in Gramps's house beside Chelsea and watched Violet carry their son, only two weeks old, to Gramps. The older man sat in his armchair.

Gramps was having a good day, and thank God for that. He was about to meet his great-grandson.

For the first time in Sam's life he would celebrate Christmas in his grandfather's house, and it felt right and good.

Sam, Violet, Chelsea and Gramps all lived here now and Sam couldn't be happier.

Yes, at some point in the future, Gramps would have to go back to the home, but not today. Not yet…

Settled into the chair that had been shaped by decades of him sitting there, Gramps held still while Violet nestled their son into his hands in his lap.

Sam and Violet, with great elation in their hearts, decided to call their son Elijah, after Violet's father, who had died too early in her life.

Sam couldn't think of a better way to honor a man his wife had loved so deeply.

"He's handsome, isn't he?" Gramps asked. "Looks like a spunky little guy to me."

"He's a baby, Gramps," Chelsea said. "He doesn't have much personality yet."

"Get over here, missy, and get to know your baby brother."

Chelsea laughed and sat on the arm of Gramps's favorite chair. She cooed at the baby and, in big-sister fashion, made sure her great-grandfather's grip on Elijah stayed secure.

Freed by Chelsea's care, Violet came over to sit beside Sam and curl against his body, her generous warmth and irrepressible personality still a revelation to him daily.

She smiled at him, her violet eyes bright with happiness. He wrapped his arm around her.

"Happy?" she asked.

"I've never been more content in my life." He tucked a curl behind her ear. "I've never felt more right. And you?"

"I'm the same. I'm so glad you came to town pretending to be something you weren't."

"And I'm glad you gave me such a hard time about it. I fell in love with you that first day, even as you frustrated the hell out of me. You were a real hard-ass."

"Get used to it," she said, laughing and flashing her wedding band at him. "I'll probably frustrate you many more times before our lives are through."

Just before he kissed her, Sam murmured, "I'm looking forward to it."

He thought back to his arrival here in Rodeo and his deep sense of loss that his heritage had been about to slip through his fingers. The past months had been special.

He'd grown to love the town.

He'd become well acquainted with his heritage.

They'd hung Violet's ultrasound in the diner.

Over the following months, everyone who had entered and had studied it had declared the tiny fetus sound and healthy looking.

Lester Voile had predicted the boy would make a

great chef someday, and Lester would share his recipes with him.

They'd all been right. Elijah was a healthy, contented baby.

An anticipated knock on the door had Chelsea casting a glance at Sam to help her out.

He went to the armchair to take Elijah from Gramps, who tired easily.

Chelsea ran to the front door to welcome the Reads.

Tori squealed and Rachel said, "Where's this baby boy I've heard so much about?"

They entered the living room of the heritage house, bringing the cold bite of winter with them, quickly vanquished by the heat from the blazing fire in the hearth.

Tori held a bottle of silver nail polish, Rachel held rosy, smiling Beth and Travis held, well, everything else.

Sam passed Elijah to Violet, and unburdened Travis of diaper bags and carriers and grocery bags that sounded like they held jars of food. In that moment, Sam saw a flash of his future, carting the paraphernalia of babyhood around for a few years to come.

Violet was adamant that they would have more than one child together. Being an only child, she wanted a big family.

Sam approved, knowing that it meant years more of parenthood in a town that had given him so much, including that very fatherhood he hadn't known he'd been dying to return to again. And he would be doing it in a town he'd grown to love with people about whom he cared deeply.

Tori barely acknowledged the baby. She and Chelsea ran upstairs to paint their nails.

"Tori and I want the wishbone. Save it for us. It's ours."

"Hey, watch the entitled 'tude, kid," Violet called.

Chelsea called back down the stairs, "I love you, too, Vy."

If Sam could have bottled the look of pleasure on his wife's face, he could sell it and make a fortune.

Rachel had traded Beth for Elijah and made a huge fuss over him.

Sam got himself and Travis a couple of beers.

Later, while everyone gathered in the kitchen to carve turkey and put out hot casserole dishes, Sam held his son.

When they sat down to dinner, he still cradled him in one arm.

"I can put him in his crib, Sam."

"I'm good, Violet." Sam kissed his son's forehead, immersing himself in the soft baby-powder scent of him.

Gramps sat at the head of the table and gave thanks for their meal, for family and friendships and for Elijah.

At the other end of the table, Sam stared down at the bundle of perfection in his arms and gave his own thanks for Violet, who confounded and completed him and who made life interesting.

While he ate one-handed with the baby tucked into his other arm, he thanked the universe for the son he'd been given.

Elijah Carson Summer Carmichael was a joy and a blessing…and a son of Rodeo, Montana.

* * * * *

*If you liked this story, check out the earlier books in
Mary Sullivan's* RODEO, MONTANA *miniseries,*
RODEO FATHER
and
RODEO RANCHER.
*And watch for more books coming later in 2017 and
2018 from Harlequin Western Romance!*

Get 2 Free Books,

HARLEQUIN®
Western Romance

Plus 2 Free Gifts—
just for trying the
Reader Service!

"What are you doing letting a Rebel into your house?" Remi
turned on her grandmother.

Miss Bertie shrugged. "I have nothing against the
Rebels."

"John Rebel killed my father. Have you forgotten that?"

Oh, *crap*. It dawned on Paxton for the first time. This had
to be Ezra McCray's daughter.

"Okay, missy, I'm not standing here and letting you paint
your father as a saint. Everyone in this town was scared of
him. And in case you've forgotten, he tried to kill two of the
Rebel boys."

"I'd rather not talk about this, and I'd rather not talk to
him." She nodded toward Paxton.

"Do you know what he's doing here?" Miss Bertie asked.

"No."

"He helped me haul my calves to the auction barn today."

"Gran—"

Paxton had had enough. He wasn't stepping into this land
mine. He handed Miss Bertie the papers. "You can pick up
your check tomorrow afternoon." He tipped his hat. "It's
been a pleasure."

"Wait a minute. I want to look at this," Miss Bertie called, and he forced himself to stop and turn around. "I have to find my glasses." She disappeared down a hallway.

Remi stepped farther into the room. "What are you doing here?"

"Your grandmother just told you. I hauled her calves to the auction."

"There was no need."

"Oh, and who was going to do it? You?"

"I could have."

"I don't think so. You're not well." The moment the words left his mouth he knew they were not something you said to a woman. And he was right. Her sea-green eyes simmered with anger.

She moved closer to him. "I'm fine. Do you hear me? I'm fine." She wagged one long finger in his face. "I'm fine."

He did the only thing a red-blooded cowboy could do. He bit her finger.

She jumped back. "You bit me!"

"I'm going to keep biting you until you admit the truth."

"You…you…stay away from my grandmother." She turned and pranced into the living room.

"A thank-you would have been nice!" he shouted to her back.

He walked out and shoved the shift of his pickup into gear, backing up and leaving the crazy ladies behind. He was sticking his nose into something that didn't concern him. And he had no desire to get to know Ezra McCray's daughter.

Don't miss TEXAS REBELS: PAXTON
by Linda Warren, available August 2017
wherever Harlequin® Western Romance
books and ebooks are sold.

www.Harlequin.com

LOVE
Harlequin romance?

Join our Harlequin community to share your thoughts and connect with other romance readers!

Be the first to find out about promotions, news, and exclusive content!

Sign up for the Harlequin e-newsletter and download a free book from any series at
www.TryHarlequin.com

CONNECT WITH US AT:

Harlequin.com/Community

Facebook.com/HarlequinBooks

Twitter.com/HarlequinBooks

Instagram.com/HarlequinBooks

Pinterest.com/HarlequinBooks

ReaderService.com

**ROMANCE WHEN
YOU NEED IT**

HSOCIAL2017